Doctors at War

A family's struggles through two World Wars

NIGEL MESSENGER

Published by Nigel Messenger in 2020

ISBN 978-1-8383569-0-3

Book Cover Design and Typeset by The Daydream Academy, Stroud, Gloucestershire.

This book is dedicated to...

All those men and women who protect us and defend our shores.

ACKNOWLEDGEMENTS

My very grateful thanks are due to my Editor Alison Jack for improving my words and texts immeasurably. She has colossal patience and attention to detail. My book is far better thanks to her valuable efforts.

Many have praised the book cover design by Jason Conway of The Daydream Academy, and I think it is a masterpiece! Thank you, Jason.

I am most grateful to members of the Cheltenham Authors Alliance who have been very helpful and generous in their advice and encouragement.

Thanks also to Brother Colin who has done some valuable research in Ireland and to all my family members for their help and support.

And of course, to my dear and very patient wife, Maura, who heroically puts up with me. I read paragraphs of my books to her enabling her to doze peacefully on the sofa.

Nigel lives in Cheltenham with his family.

CONTENTS

Introduction   1

Part One – Henry   **6**

Chapter 1   7

Salonika   7

Chapter 2   24

Henry: My Early Life   24

Chapter 3   40

Dr Jenny   40

Chapter 4   54

From Malta to London   54

Part Two – Isla   **65**

Chapter 5   66

Pins and Needles   66

Chapter 6   77

Edinburgh   77

Chapter 7   90

The Countdown to War   90

Chapter 8   102

Driving in the Blitz   102

Chapter 9   114

Leaving Home   114

Chapter 10   122

First Love   122

Part Three – Espionage   **136**

Chapter 11   137

Cruelty and Terror   137

Chapter 12   148

Horror on the Atlantic   148

Chapter 13   157

Enigma   157

Chapter 14   170

Love Blooms at Bletchley Park   170

Chapter 15   180

A Hero's Death   180

Chapter 16   190

New Hope   190

Part Four – The Forgotten Army   **204**

Chapter 17   205

Philip   205

Chapter 18   214

A Return to India   214

Chapter 19   226

A Journey into Hell   226

Chapter 20   240

The Battle Intensifies   240

Chapter 21   253

The Allies Prevail   253

Aftermath   262

Bibliography   264

INTRODUCTION

The Great War is raging across the world and the British are fighting beside their allies against the Macedonians.

In the hospitals of Malta and Salonika, two dedicated doctors are locked in an ongoing battle of their own. One, an active Suffragette trained in Edinburgh, faces a daily fight for status and respect at a time when 'lady' doctors were despised and mistrusted. The other trained in The Royal College of Surgeons in Dublin and nearby hospitals. Both are strongly opinionated and passionate about their calling; a clash of personalities is inevitable. However, love flourishes in the most adverse of conditions – the two doctors go on to set up not one but two practices in London, as well as welcoming a daughter into the world.

As time goes by, war also impacts on the lives of the doctors' descendants. Told from the point of view of various family members, the action leads the reader from the turbulent world of London during the Blitz to the code breaking genius of Bletchley Park, from the tense Battle of the Atlantic to the terrible Battle of Kohima.

Nigel Messenger is also the author of *The Miracle of Michmash*, *Meggido*, *The Battles for Armageddon*, and *From Eden to Babylon*.

The Miracle of Michmash

Two battles three thousand years apart, yet almost identical in every detail.

The British Army is facing the Turks uphill towards Michmash with high loss of life expected. The night before the battle, a British major, reading the Bible, comes across a reference to Michmash where the Israelites, under Saul and his son Jonathan, confronted a huge army of Philistines. With the odds stacked against the Israelites, Jonathan found a secret passage, enabling them to outflank the enemy and emerge triumphant. Millennia later, the British copy these tactics hoping that this mysterious and miraculous event which continues to confound historians, will repeat itself.

This book chronicles the life and experiences of Jonathan, and then fast-forwards to 1918, following the adventures of chef and soldier Bert Silverman.

Megiddo, the Battles for Armageddon

A trio of portentous historic adventures helps shape a remarkable man of the twentieth century.

At Megiddo in Palestine, the Armageddon of the Bible, three momentous battles have taken place.

Docker Nat Sullivan, fighting under Allenby during the campaign in the First World War, has vivid dreams of fighting with Richard the Lionheart in the Third Crusade, and even further back in time with the Biblical Deborah, probably one of the greatest generals of all time.

This book tells the fascinating story of Nat as he returns to the docks and rises through the Union ranks to become Deputy to the political giant and statesman, Ernest Bevan, General Secretary of the TUC. Now a Labour MP, Nat follows Ernest as he gains in power during and after World War Two.

From Eden to Babylon

A filthy barge arrives in Basra full of British soldiers. Wounded, starving, and dehydrated, most are more dead than alive.

After the British surrender at the battle of Kut, an officer and his team take the men from the barge to a steamer heading for Bombay. They are then transported by train to a hospital in the cooler Northern India. But that isn't the end of the story for the officer.

Among the survivors, he recognises one gravely wounded man who had saved his life in South Africa during the horrendous Boer War some years before. And when this man's sister travels to India from England to nurse him back to health, she is destined to fall in love with his rescuer.

In this book, the World War One action takes the reader to Mesopotamia, India, Arabia and South Africa, following the adventures of a family who work and fight together, before being reunited with their loved ones at a joyful wedding celebration.

About the Author

Nigel Messenger has spent a lifetime working in the Hospitality business and now has his own consultancy company. He has also worked for and supported the Poppy Factory, which provides employment support to wounded, injured and sick veterans, for almost thirty years.

Apart from his family, Nigel has two major passions – cricket and history. He says, "History taught in schools can be very boring for the poor recipients. People remember and relate to stories rather than dates, so my interest is in describing the effects historical events had on ordinary families."

Nigel has written four books about World War One in the Middle East. Book 4 also covers events in World War Two. The last two books were inspired by the experiences of his family members in various parts of the world.

"They were not heroes, but ordinary men and women who carried out their duties often under the most extraordinary conditions and deprivation. I have tried to be as historically accurate as possible including using the language of these times. No offence is intended".

To keep up to date with Nigel's news and books please visit nigelmessengerblog.com

Part One

Henry

CHAPTER 1

Salonika

The young soldier was caught by the vicious barbed wire hidden in the mountain stream. The more he struggled, the more entangled he became. Now he could hardly move, his whole body wrapped up in the evil snare.

As I watched him through my field glasses, my heart sank. I dreaded the jackals coming out to get him. The visualisation of such a horrible death made me shudder and I was nearly sick with horror. So pitiful was his situation, I almost hoped a sniper would shoot him to save him more agonising pain.

All the soldiers had been warned repeatedly about the dangers of hidden wires in these streams. They took the risks because it was often the quickest way up the mountain. Partially hidden in the trench formed by the running water, they believed they would become a more difficult target for the snipers, forgetting that the merciless wires would be likely to catch them instead. I had seen many men go this way and our casualties in the past few weeks had been truly horrible.

The poor boy must have been half a mile away from where we were. Could any of us get to him in time?

I had felt so helpless in the past few days, witnessing the deaths and mutilation of so many of our soldiers, and in most cases, we could do so little to help. Only yesterday, we'd retrieved the body of another soldier, hit by snipers while entangled in barbed wire.

I came to an abrupt decision. Carrying my medical bag, I walked off towards the mountain, absolutely determined to help this poor soul. My friends called out to me, urging me to come back immediately – what I was doing was strictly forbidden. There was little I could do anyway, they reasoned, and I could get myself killed as well, leaving them a doctor short in a team whose numbers were already hopelessly inadequate. But I had made my mind up.

I didn't stop to look back. Determined to save at least this one life, I carried on walking as quickly as I could across the uneven ground towards the foot of the mountain.

When I got near to the struggling soldier, I called out to him. He was whimpering in pain, his flesh cut to ribbons, and he was still wriggling, but the more he moved, the worse the cuts became. I climbed the short slope up to where he was lying and told him to stay as still as he could. To start a conversation, ensuring he was as relaxed as possible, I asked for his name. In a strained and croaking voice, he told me he was called Tom

Haslam and I gave him mine. I couldn't believe how young he looked and sounded, guessing he was little more than fifteen. Why would the authorities allow a child to join up? He should have been in school with his friends or at home with his mother. I was horrified.

I took out my cutters to try to free him and managed to remove some of the outer layers of the brutal wire. Just then, a small rock bounced down the mountainside, missing me by a couple of feet, followed by several more. I was too fired up to be afraid, too focused on my task to regret my actions. It was important to keep Tom calm so I kept on speaking to him, telling him that I would get him back home to his loved ones. He lay still as I gradually pulled the strands away.

Just then a rock hit me on the shoulder and I cried out in pain, falling back down the slope away from the boy. I was in agony, knowing the rock had probably chipped a bone, but I set to my task once again. As I climbed back up, I could hear a cheer of triumph from the thrower a couple of hundred feet above me. My involuntary cry would have told him he had scored a direct hit, but I didn't think he could see us, which was to our advantage. I had treated many men with bones bruised and broken as a result of rocks thrown by the enemy while our soldiers were hidden in gullies out of sight of the snipers. It would seem the enemy enjoyed their sport.

I carried on with my work, cutting and folding the wire back, working as fast as I could. My hands were torn and bleeding and nervous sweat poured off my head. I wiped my eyes with my sleeve to clear my vision. This was taking too long; I had to speed up my work.

I wondered how I was going to get Tom safely away as we would be sighted as soon as we left the trench. When I asked him if he thought he would be able to walk, he nodded slightly. I hoped so; I wasn't sure I was strong enough to carry him and it would be a disaster if I let him fall, but I needed to keep my worries to myself. As I worked, I kept talking to calm him, but he was openly crying in pain from the sharp thorns of wire.

At last, I folded the final wire back and eased him into a sitting position so that I could lift him up by his armpits, but he was a dead weight.

"Help me by pushing with your feet, Tom."

He didn't reply but worked his legs slowly. Between us, we managed to get him standing, but he had no strength left. With a superhuman effort, I managed to pull him away from the sharp barbs and finally we were free of the deadly stuff.

Tom slumped into unconsciousness as I slowly dragged him down the slope of the mountain. I gritted my teeth, waiting for the inevitable bullets, and sure enough, they whistled past us and cracked into the rocks near our feet. I continued to drag Tom down the mountain, but we were now exposed to the snipers.

When we got to the foot of the slope, I put one arm behind his shoulders and the other under his legs and lifted him up. My back was now exposed to the enemy. The effort was huge, and as I struggled to draw breath, the sweat poured off me. I staggered towards my friends and safety, but the distance seemed impossible. After a few steps, I collapsed. Tom groaned as he and I hit the ground.

Through my exhaustion, I could hear my friends calling out to me.

"Get up on your feet and keep going!"

"You're a sitting duck there. Move!"

With another superhuman effort, I got to my feet again and lifted Tom up, managing to stagger a few feet forward before collapsing again. I got up and lurched forward one more time. The bullets were whistling past me far too close; I knew I could be hit at any moment.

Then the inevitable happened. I heard the smack of a bullet and felt a horrible pain in my back.

Collapsing to the ground, I was vaguely aware of my friends running towards me and calling out.

Then I remembered nothing more.

I became dimly aware of misty figures passing across my vision. A voice was speaking.

"You were bloody lucky, Smythson! We managed to remove the bullet from your back. Luckily it hadn't gone too far in."

My back was aching with pain and my whole body felt as if I had run a marathon. Eventually, I managed to drift off into a deep slumber. When I next awoke, I was feeling a little fresher.

The same voice carried on from where it had left off earlier.

"You were bloody lucky to bump into a bunch of quacks who managed to save your life. You're in a lot of bloody trouble for disobeying orders and running off like that. Mind you, if it was up to me, you'd be getting a bloody great medal for rescuing that boy. He was dead for sure in that stream, wrapped up in that bloody wire. We counted more than forty wounds on him – some of them so deep, they needed stitches."

"Will he survive?" I croaked with great effort, still in fierce pain. By now I had recognised the voice as belonging to orderly Bill Martin who had been with our group since we had set sail from Malta.

"Survive? He's already crying out for food – and drink, too. You'd think he'd had enough in that bloody stream. I've known big bloody elephants eat and drink less."

Bill was a fine one to talk – he was carrying at least thirty unnecessary pounds, a big bulging stomach showing above his thick belt. On a better day, I would have retorted that he was the one who needed to improve his lifestyle, but now I wanted information from him. Besides, underneath the pasty face and the bluff manner, Bill was a good man.

"Was my wound serious?" I asked.

"Still bloody alive, aren't you? The bullet just missed your spine so you should be able to walk, but we won't know till you try. We had to put stitches in your hands and treat the small wound in your shoulder from that bloody rock which hit you. I'll get Dr Edmund over later to give you a better idea about your bullet wound. Anything you want?"

"No, just sleep."

When I woke later, there were three of my colleagues standing over me. They were trying to be cheerful but couldn't hide their worries, their faces strained with concern. Dr Edmund was the senior man there and a good friend.

"We hope you will be able to walk, but we need to give you more tests to check for internal damage. Can you get on to your feet and show us what you can do?" he asked.

He and the others lifted the bedclothes and helped me to slide my legs to the floor. I was in terrible pain – mainly from the bullet wound, but I ached all over, so it was hard to be sure. My shoulder was very stiff and caused me huge discomfort.

My colleagues supported my arms until I was half standing, but try as I might, I could not move my legs nor even support myself. They were very patient with me as I made another huge effort to move, but I was unable to. I felt pathetic and helpless.

They laid me back on the bed.

The following day was just as hopeless. I dreaded spending the rest of my life in a wheelchair, dependent on others for every human need. I would have to go back to the family home in Ireland. No! That would be the end of my life. I had to get back on my feet and walk.

"What's the verdict?" I asked Edmund.

"We need to get you back to base where we have proper facilities. I'm afraid the journey will be rather uncomfortable and will take a few days, but as you know, we have teams of dedicated nurses and doctors there as well as operating theatres, although we are still desperately short of medicines and equipment.

"By the way, you won't be put on a charge for your reckless behaviour, but an officer came to tell us that the next idiot who tries a similar stunt will be court marshalled. We thought you were incredibly brave, though."

I felt a bit better after that and was very grateful to my friends.

Since the order to attack had been given, our medical team had been inundated with casualties: limbs torn off, guts and brains spilling out, and endless horrible wounds from the barbed wire. I couldn't remember the number of times men had begged me to finish them off so that they would suffer no more, and in some hopeless cases, that's exactly what I and the rest of the medical team had to do. To save one person from carrying the inevitable guilt that comes from ending a life, even when it's the only humane thing to do, we always consulted as a team before we gave the final injection.

We could barely cope with the high number of casualties, which seemed to be increasing every day, sending as many back to Salonika as we could. There was always the risk that the journey, largely by mule and partly by rickety ambulance on the makeshift roads, might cause them more harm than good, but we were desperately short of medicines and medical equipment and constantly begging our senior officers to get more supplies. We lost hundreds of men while they were suffering unnecessary pain and blood loss as we didn't even have the basic bandages to staunch the flow.

What a contrast to our situation a few short weeks ago; we had been based in the huge camp just outside Salonika in an area known as the Birdcage, protected by miles of barbed wire rolled into deadly waves just to the north of us. Our camp contained thousands of people, mainly French and British soldiers together with huge civilian support. An enormous tented hospital with miles of corridors and vast wards staffed by a large army of nurses treated our casualties.

Many of our patients were suffering from malaria. Already rife in that part of the world, it was exacerbated by our somewhat primitive hygiene arrangements. We spent much of our time cleansing our streams and water sources to minimise the disease; although malaria is rarely life-threatening, it could bring armies to a halt as soldiering duties were out of the question for most of the victims.

One of the men described malaria symptoms as feeling like electric shocks shooting through his legs, body and head, along with excruciating headaches and severe body chills, and many sufferers found it difficult to control their movements. For treatment, we often used quinine tablets or, in extreme cases, injections of a quinine solution. This would effectively kill the parasites in the blood, but often they were replaced by a new supply of parasites and the symptoms reoccurred. Our medical stocks were always low and replacements hindered by the devastating activities of the U-boats which had blown hundreds of tons of supplies to the bottom of the ocean, together with thousands of our precious people.

Our war situation was in stalemate: we were here to support our friends the Serbians who were being threatened by the Bulgarians and other powers, but we had arrived too late and Serbia had fallen. Meanwhile, the Bulgarians had made a strong fortress over many months on the top of the steep mountains to the north of us. With their knowledge of the country and superior training, we had no hope of attacking and overcoming them, so we were sitting in Salonika, waiting with our allied armies.

Life was very boring and no one knew what was going to happen. That was, until a Member of Parliament asked a question in the House of Commons relating to our inactivity. Why was Britain tying up so many resources in Salonika when other theatres of war were desperate for men and equipment? The government was put under pressure to demand action leading to a solution in Macedonia.

This latest slaughter, therefore, was due once again to the stupidity and recklessness of British politicians. They really had no idea what was going on, but under pressure from the public (who also had no idea), they had commanded our forces to fight against an impregnable high fortress. Meanwhile, the Member of Parliament who started all this with his ill-considered question probably went back to his suburban home in his laundered clothes, living comfortably with his family in blissful ignorance of the mass culling of our forces he had brought about. This made me burn with incandescent rage and impotency, but we had to obey and march forward.

Our party of around a dozen doctors had a similar number of soldiers to protect us. We took several days travelling over rough and stony ground and steep mountains on horseback, followed by large numbers of pack mules as motor transport could barely cope with the narrow passages and muddy streams. These mules were comical animals who would often prance and dance until their packs came loose. At this point, they deposited their loads on the paths, which could hold up the whole column for many minutes. While we were cursing, the mules brayed at us in triumph, the hilarious noises they made sounding for all the world like raucous laughter.

The weather was mostly kind to us but became blisteringly hot as time went on, and of course we were bitten to bits by the mosquitoes. Macedonia was an extremely poor country and we saw miserable and hungry people living in dirty hovels as their villages had been devastated in the recent Balkan wars. Wild dogs seemed to rule the land, barking fiercely at us and showing their teeth. The land was bleak and desolate.

This was the terrain I had to be taken across, weak and injured from my recklessly brave rescue of Tom, on the journey back to base. The army had given our party a wagon and horses so I could lie down under cover, but we had to take an awfully long way round to find a flat enough route. Edmund hadn't been joking about the journey; those few days were some of the worst of my life. I felt every twist and bump in the road and struggled not to cry out. I prayed for the wagon and horses to stop for a break, but the long spells carried on almost beyond my endurance. Worried that my wounds had worsened, I still had no feeling in my back and legs, and was terrified for my future prospects. The pain got worse, and on the rougher paths, I lost consciousness several times. The heat was indescribable.

I was so relieved finally to wake up back in the hospital tent within the huge area of the Birdcage just north of the city of Salonika, surrounded by miles of barbed wire. The Birdcage protected us from enemy incursions and allowed us to develop a vast community, almost a new city within its boundaries.

I had, of course, worked in this hospital for a few months until my medical services were needed to help the men on the frontline. The dormitories were huge with rows of beds and short gaps between them. My ward was full of many different types of casualties, the majority being malaria sufferers, and now there were more and more wounded coming in from the front as our army moved forward to climb the heights in the vain hope of unseating the Bulgarians. Our casualty rates were huge as our men were exposed at the foot of the mountains. Many said that they felt like sitting ducks, unable to fight back effectively.

To begin with, I felt too poorly to communicate with those either side of me, preferring my own misery. It seemed strange to be the patient here now after having been one of the doctors; I definitely preferred being upright rather than prone!

Then gradually, I got to know my neighbours. The man on my right had bullet wounds from running on to machine guns set into the hills. He was lucky to have been rescued but must have suffered terribly on the long journey back. I didn't think he felt much like talking; I heard him crying softly through the night and I decided it was better to leave him be, but eventually he became more communicative.

"I fought in the trenches in France for several months," he told me. "The conditions were awful; we were living in mud and were wet and cold just about all the time. I didn't realise how awful things would be when we signed up, and if I had known, I would have thought twice about it. I don't think we were even achieving anything there. I was eventually evacuated back to England to recover from having breathed in some horrible green gas. And then was sent out here as punishment, or so it feels. What's the point of all this anyway?"

Like Tom, he was very young and missing home desperately. Looking at his injuries, I wasn't optimistic about his chances. I felt so very sorry for him.

The man on my left had a broken leg, but I was unsure exactly what had happened to him.

"My wife and I run a small butcher's shop in Yorkshire which we inherited from her parents," he said, another one missing home, it seemed. "It's not much but keeps us alive. I am really worried about how she will manage without me, especially as we have two small children to look after. If she can't manage the shop, then she will have very little to live on. I hope I can get back to her soon."

His Yorkshire accent was strong and I sometimes had difficulty following his words, although he probably had the same problem with my Irish brogue. Talking to these two injured young men, I despaired about all the lives which had been wrecked by this dreadful war and hoped it would be over soon. All these poor people wanted was to get back to their families and some kind of normality.

The dormitory became so hot some days, we all sweated uncomfortably. The smells of too many humans cramped together was almost unbearable, until the nurses took pity on us and opened up the tent flaps to let in the fresh air which helped a little.

By this time, I was able to move around in my bed, but was not confident enough to put my legs on to the floor. My back still hurt appallingly, and I felt drained by my ordeal and the long, uncomfortable journey back to base. During endless boring hours in my bed, my mind would wander and I spent much of my time thinking about my life so far.

CHAPTER 2

Henry: My Early Life

My name is Henry Smythson. I was born in 1880 in Ireland, the fourth son of Thomas and Sarah Smythson who produced eight boys and four girls. The fourteen of us lived happily in a modest house in the village of Abbeyleix in County Laois, roughly in the middle of the country. Families of that size were the norm in those days, although I can't for the life of me remember where we all slept.

My father was a policeman in the Royal Irish Constabulary, and all my brothers joined him there. I was the only boy in our family who had no interest at all in following the working tradition. We were a Protestant family and Protestants made up a quarter of police numbers. Life was much more relaxed in the countryside; it was only later that I would encounter the prejudices and religious conflicts in the cities and in the north. In Abbeyleix, we lived side by side, Protestants and Catholics, just ordinary Irish people with the same rights.

I enjoyed my schooldays. A bright, hard-working student, I managed to divide my time between studies and playing sports. I also loved horses, and whenever I had time, I rode on my uncle's estate. Occasionally, I followed the hunt – this was a time when field sports were a natural and essential part of country life in Ireland.

After reading books about the life and times of Victorian doctors, many of whom became missionaries in Africa, I was determined to join the medical profession. These brave men and women were my role models – I was astounded by their commitment and bravery, and moved by those who made the ultimate sacrifice. I often wondered if I could live up to their extraordinary standards of humanity.

My family were supportive of my ambitions, although it was doubtful whether they'd have the resources to fund them. However, I studied hard, and when I eventually won a scholarship to The Royal College of Surgeons, I was supported by some of the wealthier members of my extended family.

My first visit to Dublin was frightening. It took me several months to get used to the bustling city after my quiet rural upbringing and I missed my family terribly. Even with their generous support, money was tight and I remember having to forgo several meals. Going drinking was out of the question. However, the work totally absorbed me and I soaked up my medical training with great relish.

After I qualified, I worked as the resident surgeon at Dr Steevens' Hospital in Kilmainham. I had heard about its great reputation for healing all comers without prejudice, a principle I was passionate about. The hospital had the best medical library in Dublin, so my new position suited me very well. I worked hard, covering long hours, but I was content.

One day, just as I was going to visit a patient, one of my doctor friends stopped me in the corridor.

"Come on, Henry, it's time for you to have a change of scene. You've been working non-stop since I've known you, and you never went out when we were students. You'll become boring!"

"I didn't have the money to go out as a student, and now I don't have the time," I replied, rather primly.

"That's crazy! You must make time for fun. Good God, man, you can afford it! You are earning your own money now. Listen, I'm playing the banjo in a band in Mulligans this Saturday. I'll expect to see you there. It's a great craic."

I had never been to a Dublin pub before, but I couldn't resist the invitation. With a couple of other doctors and a few of the nurses, the music, drinking and dancing pouring out into the street, I had the best night of my life so far. After this, I realised what I had been missing. We went out regularly from then on, getting to know the traditional Dublin pubs, a great and well-deserved relaxation after all my hard work.

Sometimes, however, our socialising got out of hand. Some of my friends could drink and party all night, and go straight back to the hospital for their next shift, but that was beyond me. After having had difficulty getting up for work a few times, I learnt not to keep up with the others, but to carry on at my own pace.

We all knew that war was coming, and I was keen to support our soldiers when it did, so I applied to join the Royal Army Medical Corps (RAMC) at the Portobello Hospital, Dublin. While I was there, I decided to specialise in treating venereal diseases as these were prevalent amongst the young soldiers and I hated to see them suffer so. These diseases debilitated thousands of men and I regarded it as my duty to reduce the infections and find ways to eliminate them.

"Why don't you do some research into Salvarsan?" a colleague asked me. "Early results have been very promising, but the drug needs more thorough testing. If it has potential, you could create a special study and perhaps make a big difference for our soldiers and others."

This was an excellent suggestion! I immediately started work to find out more, launching a research project to evaluate the drug's effectiveness. Early studies were indeed extremely promising: Salvarsan helped to eliminate bad bacteria without damaging the person, although there were side effects.

I was enormously proud to have two papers on the use of this drug published. Having added valuable information to the vast empirical data on the subject, I decided I would continue my research for the rest of my life, whatever form it took.

I was also trained as a radiographer. This involved operating a bulky machine which enabled us to look inside a patient's body to identify illnesses and diseases, as well as looking for foreign objects. Radiology was a new science with tremendous potential to improve medical practice in peacetime as well as in war. Early pioneers discovered that some elements, such as uranium, could produce rays which passed through the body, exposing the bones and other solids hidden beneath.

The magnificent Marie Curie devoted most of her lifetime to developing this technology, seeing the potential for its use in war and providing mobile units powered by vehicle engines which were so useful to field hospitals. Later, my colleagues and I would use the technology to find the exact position of bullets and shrapnel inside the wounded, enabling us to carry out surgery with precision and without unnecessary cutting. Thousands of lives were saved on the battlefields – but then, if human beings didn't start wars in the first place, even more lives would be saved. Sadly, having dedicated her life to the saving of others, Marie Curie eventually died from exposure to radiation.

I was delighted to be made a Captain in the RAMC. Before I left Ireland, I was even happier to have the opportunity to visit my family in Abbeyleix.

My mother answered the door, her face shining with joy.

"Henry, you look so smart and important in your beautiful new uniform. You have such a responsible position and we are all so proud of you."

My parents were especially pleased that a member of the family had finally broken away from the working tradition and become a doctor, hoping that my younger brothers and sisters would think about studying for a profession, too. Mother cooked her special Irish stew; I never did find out her recipe. Although I have tried to replicate her delicious dish on many occasions, I've never had the same success.

Within months of my return to Dublin, I was ordered to board a ship to Malta. Twenty doctors had been selected to travel together, managing to avoid the German U-boats and eventually arriving safely in the Port of Valletta in Malta in 1914. This was my first time on the water, and despite my intense fear of attack, I loved the experience.

Many hospitals had been built in Malta to look after the wounded from Egypt and Palestine, and later from our disastrous conflict in the Dardanelles. The thousands of cases of malaria coming in meant we needed to create more space to accommodate the victims of this debilitating disease and more staff were called from home.

After a busy few months working in two of the hospitals, I was one of the people called into a meeting by the Colonel.

"We will all move to Salonika to tend to the sick and wounded there. We are desperately needed closer to the front to treat malaria patients and get them back into action. U-boat activity has increased and we don't want to lose any more wounded men by transporting them here."

So it's OK for us to risk our lives travelling there, I thought rather cynically. But overall, this made good sense to us and we looked forward to our new adventure. I was worried about the U-boat threat, though.

We left the following Sunday. After a long sea journey, once again dodging the many U-boats which commanded the waters, we reached the Greek coast. Fortunately, we arrived safely, but many did not; when we were about ten miles out from the harbour, we heard a tremendous boom and saw a massive flash of fire in the distance, followed by a long spiral of black smoke which trailed high into the heavens. As we came closer to Salonika, there was little left of the SS *Marquette*, just the flotsam and jetsam of a once great ship: rough pieces of wood, dented cans, patches of burning oil and scraps of clothing. The ship had disappeared completely and what was left of it was now at the bottom of the ocean.

I admit I cried for the hundreds of wasted human and animal lives and the terror they must have felt, hopefully very briefly. We had also lost valuable medical supplies, grain and vehicles. We were all quiet and thoughtful as our ship coasted into Salonika harbour. In my distress, I hardly noticed the famous round tower with its medieval battlements and the colourful little houses spilling down the hillside.

We were picked up by several Ford ambulances, which the drivers called Tin Lizzie's, taking us the short distance through the city to our base within the vast area known as the Birdcage. Still in shock from the dreadful devastation we had witnessed on our arrival, we started our work looking after the sick servicemen.

As we had discovered in Malta, malaria was the most common illness, outnumbering battle casualties many times over. Dysentery was also common and extremely serious, but the condition I became interested in was known as shell shock. I was keen to help the men who suffered the most enormous stress from a condition that was barely recognised by the senior ranks, but we certainly acknowledged its reality, and we had heard that the thousands of men coming back from the trenches were also suffering from this affliction. I heard it referred to as 'war neurosis' and 'combat fatigue' amongst other names. The symptoms included nightmares, depression and acute anxiety, and later I discovered many others in the men I treated. Some had fierce headaches and dizziness, while others suffered sight, hearing and memory loss.

Fascinated to know more, I went to a lecture about the condition. A doctor who had served in France began his talk with:

"Officers are much more likely to suffer from shell shock as they try to suppress their emotions in front of their men. There is no doubt this condition is real and many thousands at the front have been affected. Some of these men have been sent to mental hospitals in England, and in several cases, they have been shot for cowardice.

"Many of my colleagues don't understand this illness and have subsequently grossly mistreated the victims. In the worst cases, I have heard electric shock therapy and solitary confinement have been inflicted. We need to educate our doctors and train them to treat the condition. Unfortunately, there are huge gaps in our knowledge, and we need more research into this condition."

I was horrified to hear this and determined to find out more to help these poor men. Over time, I learnt that we doctors had to build up a strong bond of trust with individual sufferers, and some of us practised forms of psychotherapy, explanation, suggestion and persuasion to relieve their symptoms. Other doctors were keener on massage, warm baths and light exercise for the sufferers. I believed that we must treat the whole person, so a combination of physical and mental support was needed.

We made some progress, but not a great deal. There was no doubt in my mind that after the war was over, major research was required into this terrible condition.

I was also able to practise my research interest into venereal diseases, which afflicted a good number of our men. The City of Salonika was only a short distance away and one senior doctor called it a 'den of iniquity'. The city was dirty and full of disease – not a good place to spend too much time.

Troops from many countries roamed the streets; as well as British and French, there were soldiers from China, Senegal, Russia and more. There was a confused mixture of religions: Jews, Mohammedans and neutral Greeks. Gossip about spies from every nation pervaded the many bars and cafés.

Inevitably, the city was a magnet for hundreds of prostitutes. Our soldiers made several visits to these women, mainly to relieve the boredom of camp, and many brought back diseases. Some colleagues took me there once and I was dazzled by the kaleidoscope of colours and nationalities and huge numbers of people in vibrant clothes. I saw the numerous fruits, vegetables and spices of the markets, most of which I had never heard of before. Certainly, Salonika was even livelier than Dublin!

My friends took me to a dark and dingy club in a basement where soldiers sat at tables, watching and listening to a lady singer of uncertain nationality and age. She didn't seem to hear the beat from the band behind her and sang at her own pace; she had either imbibed too much of the inferior whisky served here or was on a substance somewhat more potent.

My colleagues enjoyed the surroundings and atmosphere while I did not. I was relieved when we left and emerged into the bright, warm air. Immediately, I bumped into a young lady who, in poor English, invited me to visit her in a nearby building. I refused, of course, preferring to get back to the familiarity and security of our camp.

And so, my life story brought me eventually to lie wounded in a hospital bed in the Birdcage. One of the nurses in the hospital, Niamh, was particularly friendly and kind. She told me she was from Ireland, by coincidence only a few miles from my home, and let me know how she came to be here.

"I wanted to help soldiers in the war, and a friend and I found out that we could become nurses. We had to move to England for training, and eventually we qualified and joined the Queen Alexandra Imperial Military Nursing Service. This is our first posting, and we expect to stay here."

Niamh was a fine-looking Irish colleen with shining black hair and lively eyes. She and her colleagues looked very smart in their grey uniforms with white starched caps and polished shoes, and they were a huge asset to the medical team, providing a great boost to our wellbeing and recovery. They had their downsides, though.

"Come along now, Doctor, it's time for your bed bath." Niamh delivered this as 'good news'. She and the other nurses helped to make life bearable for us patients, but we could have done without the indignity of the bed baths!

To take my mind off being so helpless, I asked Niamh what life was like for the nurses working in the Birdcage.

"We do most of the work," she explained as she carefully wiped down my arms and chest. "In addition to the nursing, we are responsible for adding more tents and corridors to the hospital, which takes up a lot of our time. We also have to keep all the equipment working so we are becoming excellent electrical, lighting and plumbing engineers. It seems that every day another machine is banjaxed," it was lovely to hear the Irish expressions again, "but life is good and we are so pleased to be helping you all here."

It occurred to me then that we owed a huge debt to these women. I was pleased to have such kind and committed people at this low time in my life, although I did become quite depressed and sorry for myself, despite trying really hard to remain positive. I felt as if I was falling into the swirling evil depths of a black pit, as real to me as the people in the ward. As I peered into the slimy mess, I felt my whole being slipping and sliding into oblivion. I was being sucked in and tried desperately to find something to grip to prevent my descent. If I fell, I would lose my body and mind for ever. I was as terror stricken as if I had been locked into a lions' den with no way out.

As a doctor, I was well aware of my demons; I had treated many soldiers in distress with acute depression, but I'd had no idea until now how real it could be with such tangible horrors. In better moments, I thought about my future – that is, if I ever got out of this awful situation alive and well. I wanted to continue to work as a doctor, but I didn't want to go back home to practise; I could learn much more by working and continuing my studies abroad. I decided that the best place would be London, but I needed to get fit and back on my feet first.

We were never short of news on the ward, although supplies were scarce, except for the food we were able to produce ourselves, as our ships were still struggling to get through to the harbour. Only last week, the dreaded U-boats had claimed another victim as one of our ships hit the bottom of the ocean, together with hundreds of soldiers, nurses and doctors.

Most days, we enjoyed a tasty soup with bread, followed by chicken with fresh vegetables from the Birdcage gardens. Hundreds of chickens were bred nearby so we had delicious eggs, too. These foods were good for helping to restore our health and wellbeing.

Many men and women had been here for so long that extreme boredom had led them to develop their hobbies, and gardening and animal husbandry were the most popular. They were able to grow almost all the vegetables we were familiar with from home, and we also enjoyed beautiful floral displays in the dormitories. One man had built a pigsty, and on special days we feasted on delicious pork with crackling.

Then there were the visitors, who added a little variety to an otherwise mind-numbing existence. One afternoon, I was woken by an extremely glamorous woman walking through the dormitory. She smiled at us, swaying and dancing, looking like an actress from the Victorian stage with long flowing dress and coiffured hair. She had a beautiful voice and sang some of the popular songs of the time.

My neighbour on the left, in a rare moment of communication, told me that she was a bint.

"What the hell is a bint?" I asked naively.

"Well, the lady you see before you is in fact a man."

I didn't believe a word of it. He was insistent.

"I have seen several of them here before. These are soldiers from the amateur dramatic society who dress up for their parts as women, rather like they did in the pantomimes we enjoyed as children. The better ones are minor celebrities. I thought he was very good indeed, and he certainly had you fooled!"

I'd had no idea before how hugely popular stage shows were in the Birdcage, attracting hundreds of enthusiastic fans. But when the 'woman' came over to us, smiling and chatting, I turned my head away, pretending to be asleep. I wasn't impressed with her/him at all.

A female doctor – or rather, 'lady doctor' was the term used then (and this woman really *was* a woman) – would visit me every morning. I knew that a group of lady doctors had arrived from Malta recently and I was delighted we had some new assistants, but some of my colleagues were not so pleased. They didn't believe that women were capable of being doctors, but I didn't share that prejudice. However, my first experience of being treated by a lady doctor wasn't to be one I would remember with much affection. More like terror, actually...

CHAPTER 3

Dr Jenny

"Pull those bedclothes back, man!"

She had a sharp, rather shrill voice with a strong accent which I didn't recognise at first. It later occurred to me that she was Scottish, and I guessed she was one of the Suffragette women who had caused so much trouble in Edinburgh. So I'd read in the papers, the police and prison officers had had big problems dealing with them. I personally had nothing against lady doctors, nor Suffragettes; in fact, I could see no reason why women couldn't have the vote and equality in all walks of life, but I was glad they were not all like this one.

She pulled the bedclothes from my grasp.

"Leave me alone!" I muttered. I didn't want to shout too loud and cause a fuss, but equally, I didn't want her tormenting me.

"Turn over, man, and let me look at your back." She helped me turn on to my front, and then pulled up my pyjama top. I gasped as she poked and prodded my back with her strong fingers, feeling completely humiliated. She touched my shoulder and I jumped, gasping in pain from the sensitive bruise the stone had caused, but she didn't apologise for the discomfort she'd caused me.

It occurred to me that perhaps she didn't know I was also a doctor. Doctors weren't separated from the other patients, although my name and rank were on the board at the end of my bed. She'd probably only read my listed ailments.

She pulled my bedclothes back to the end of the bed and I was terrified she was going to take down my pyjama trousers while I was still lying on my front. I felt a sharp pain in my foot and cried out in alarm; I knew what she was up to, and why.

"There's no reason why you can't walk. There's enough feeling there." She beckoned to a passing nurse with a wave of her arm. Between them, they turned me back over, eased my legs on to the floor and held my arms to pull me upright. With their help, I tried to stand and was pleased that I was almost able to. I moved my legs, but could only manage a rather feeble step with huge difficulty.

"Well, that's some progress, I suppose, but you'll have to try harder. You must make more effort."

I don't know how I managed to control my Irish temper, but it was with great difficulty. I am calm by nature and it takes a monster to make me lose it, and now I had met one! However, secretly I was thrilled as her forceful action had made me realise that I could and would walk again. She was right, but I didn't want to let her know that; she would probably never let me forget it. I resolved to ask

Niamh and her colleagues to get me practising across the ward when the lady doctor was not around.

"You are not eating enough. I will instruct the nurses on your new diet, and make sure you keep to it, Dr Smythson."

So she did know my name!

Within a couple of weeks, I was able to cross the ward with help and encouragement from Niamh. This was the hardest struggle of my life and I felt like giving up several times, but always kept the prize in mind: I *would* walk again. And I found out the name of the fearsome lady doctor from Niamh, too: Dr Jenny Park Walter. I am sure she was briefed by the nurses on my progress; in fact, she had probably instructed them on their part in my recovery.

Within a few weeks, I was moving unaided, but only slowly; it was more of a shuffle than a walk. When Dr Jenny came to check on me again, of course she had something to say on the matter.

"You need to get your confidence back. I want to see you walking with your head held high and your arms swinging, legs striding forward with crisp steps. Come on, let's see what you can do."

Good God, this woman was ruthless and relentless. Once again, I found my anger rising. I took a deep breath and managed to hold back my aggression, but I turned to my bed, deciding to do no more while she was there. She soon stormed off, sighing noisily.

Dr Jenny didn't come back for some days, and extraordinarily, I found I was missing her visits. She was a very unusual woman, stronger than most men I knew, with a sharp intellect and extensive medical knowledge, and I was finding her rather fascinating. I'd despised her voice initially, but I was growing to like the way she spoke, and her accent was softer than I'd first realised.

What's more, she was really quite attractive. I hadn't noticed her rich, long auburn hair before as she'd scraped it back into a rather harsh bun, and I really wanted to see it released. Her face was strong with almost translucent skin, but youthful and attractive, and a vague but pleasant scent of lavender emanated from her. I imagined her as a modern-day Boudicca, with armies of men worshipping at her feet.

Despite all that, she was still a monster and I really didn't want to like her. She was a rude bully with a terrible bedside manner. But she had managed to get me on to my feet and I was impressed by the way she had survived what must have been a very tough apprenticeship in Edinburgh.

I pinched myself in case I was imagining my feelings, closing my eyes tightly and then opening them to see if I had become deranged. I hadn't.

Dr Jenny had an impressive number of letters after her name, MB ChB, which meant that she was a Bachelor of Medicine as well as a Bachelor of Surgery. I had never heard of a lady doctor with both of those qualifications; it would have been impressive for a man. What an extraordinary woman!

I called my Irish friend over.

"Niamh, what do you know about Dr Jenny?" I asked.

"Well, sir, she is the talk of the whole Birdcage. She is fiercely supportive of women's rights and the rumour is that she used to be a Suffragette." I knew it! "I know a lot of people think they were just a nuisance, but in Edinburgh, the lady doctors just wanted to be treated on equal terms with their male colleagues. They were also fighting for votes for women. A just cause, if you ask me."

Dr Jenny Park Walter had just gone up several notches in my estimation. Niamh went on.

"She doesn't take any nonsense from any man. She really shouted at the Colonel yesterday in his office, and we could hear every word through the tent."

"What was she angry about?" I asked.

"Well, she and the other lady doctors are furious that they have no real status. They have no rank or uniform, and however long they have been practising, they are still junior to the youngest private here. We all think she is absolutely right and fully support her. I think she is wonderful."

Niamh's eyes were shining brightly with admiration for Dr Jenny. "Did you know," she went on, "they are not even allowed to have their clothes laundered because they are not uniforms, but they are not allowed to wear uniforms? She is dead right in calling this a ridiculous situation."

My admiration went up even further.

"I know she has another meeting with the Colonel tomorrow. Why don't you come with me to listen? We can join the regular audience eavesdropping outside."

How could I resist that offer?

At the appointed time, a crowd of about a dozen doctors and nurses gathered outside the Colonel's office. It wasn't long before we were rewarded.

"And another thing," I heard Dr Jenny say in her crisp and clear brogue, "I found out yesterday that your officers are censoring our letters home. This is outrageous! How dare you! I demand that you stop this despicable practice immediately. On whose orders has this been sanctioned? I demand to know!"

She was almost shouting at him in her strong unforgiving Edinburgh accent. I was hugely impressed while feeling a shade of sympathy for the beleaguered man.

"This has been sanctioned by Mr Churchill himself," he replied in a rather reedy voice. He didn't sound very confident.

"Then if you are afraid to stand up to him, I can assure you that I am most definitely not. I look forward to giving him a good piece of my mind when I have the opportunity. And by the way, I can't help but notice that Churchill is beginning to put on weight. Not good for him. He drinks far too much and never seems to stop smoking those smelly and dangerous cigars.

"If you do not forbid the scandalous and atrocious censorship of our letters with immediate effect, I refuse to work. And all the lady doctors here will side with me. We will, of course, continue to look after our poor men, but we will not take any orders from you or your chinless pipsqueaks."

There was a quiet pause, then, "Well, what is your answer?"

"This is being done for security reasons and is out of my jurisdiction…"

"Nonsense! That's such a stupid answer and not worthy of you. You are in charge here and your authority overrules others. You can't fool me! If you don't rescind the order immediately, I will do it myself. I will write to the Medical Woman's Federation, the BMA and, of course, Churchill himself. I will cause you so much trouble, you will deeply regret not cooperating with me. Well, what's it to be?"

"Oh, very well, Dr Walter, you leave me little choice. This practice will cease with immediate effect."

What a magnificent woman! We all felt like clapping and cheering, but it was more sensible to keep quiet. But we were already looking forward to future episodes.

A couple of weeks later, Dr Jenny came to see me.

"It's time you got up and went back to work. We don't have a radiographer here at the moment and need someone immediately. We can't look after these men properly without finding out what nasty things there are inside them."

She was quite right, as always. We needed to find the exact position of bullets and shrapnel and, of course, where the broken bones were. I could have done with at least a few more days of rest and recuperation, but I knew how determined she was and didn't feel strong enough to stand up to her.

I returned to work as she suggested, but to begin with only for the first half of the day. My colleagues were supportive and gave me all the assistance they could; I was walking, but only slowly and with difficulty. But after a time, I made a complete recovery and was able to work a full day again.

I didn't see Dr Jenny again in the Birdcage. I learnt with great sorrow that she had been sent back to Malta, travelling with several other lady doctors. The word was that her departure had nothing to do with her outbursts, but would have happened anyway. However, I am sure our Colonel breathed a sigh of relief!

A few months later, our seniors decided that as the threat of the U-boats had lessened, we should now return to care for the wounded and sick in Malta. Once back in Valetta, I was assigned to the Spinola Hospital until it closed, then I was sent to the Forrest Hospital. Here we treated, amongst others, many syphilis sufferers who had become infected in Egypt.

On my first day, I was told that all doctors were to meet in the dining room for drinks and dinner. This sounded very civilised. It had taken me a long time to feel that I belonged in medical circles and could hold my head up in the company of doctors.

When I joined my colleagues around a solid oak dining table, I was shocked to see Dr Jenny sitting opposite me, deeply engrossed in conversation with the tall man next to her. She didn't see me, or perhaps she ignored me on purpose, while I listened carefully to their discussion.

"But, Captain Douglas, you must understand that Homer was the greatest poet of all. His *Iliad* and *Odyssey* are magnificent, and Aristotle, though also a master, couldn't hold a candle to him. I studied both of these poets as a child and I know what I'm talking about…"

The poor fellow didn't stand a chance against her.

My neighbour asked about my day and I lost the thread of Dr Jenny's conversation. I was in the middle of telling him how one of my patients had had a minor seizure when a strident female voice with a strong Edinburgh accent called across the table.

"Doctor, our first rule at dinner is no talking shop. You must now buy all of us a drink. Mine's a Bristol Cream – and yours, Captain Douglas," she asked, turning to the tall man on her left, "what will that be?"

Douglas, who was looking at me rather smugly, demanded a large scotch with a small splash of soda water. I despised him in that moment, with his supercilious angular face. I then heard the pompous ass say, "Now, everyone, what's your poison? Tell the young man over there. It's his round. Don't make it too cheap, ha-ha, what-ho!"

One by one, they called out their orders to me. After four, I had to ask for a notepad and pencil as I was forgetting what each person had said, and in truth, I wasn't too familiar with some of the drinks and needed everyone to confirm. I don't think I have ever felt more embarrassed and humiliated in all my life, and I was struggling to keep my blood from rising. However, I was determined to keep control of my emotions and was furious with myself when I started blushing like a child. My face was burning. In fact, the more I tried to stop it, the worse it became.

That damned woman! She always seemed to have the advantage. Why did she annoy me so much? Was it because I was afraid that she was intellectually superior to me and a better doctor? No, this wouldn't have mattered to me at all. I was determined not to let her attitude get to me. Perhaps I was really annoyed at that blasted Captain and the way she had encouraged him.

I had heard of this Douglas fellow before and none of the stories about him were complimentary. In fact, he was known as a bully and his medical skills were well below par. When he made a mistake, he would blame someone else, often a doctor more junior than he was. He also had a reputation for fondling the nurses and used his seniority to avoid any repercussions. Not a very savoury character.

I used to start work very early in the morning, doing my rounds of the many wards I was assigned to, and I had become concerned about the lack of progress of a young Lance Corporal. He had been wounded in his left thigh, and before he arrived here from Salonika, his leg had become infected. He had received the usual treatment, but hadn't responded well.

I soon realised that his condition was worsened by his mental state; he was extremely depressed. As I knew a bit about this from my own experience, it had become apparent to me that, as with so many other patients, he needed treatment for his depression before he was going to get better. So, I spent some time every day talking and listening to him, using skills I had learnt in Salonika.

When I arrived on the ward one morning, I saw Dr Jenny standing over him. A nurse stood at the other side of the bed and between them they were examining his infected leg. Dr Jenny frowned as she bent lower, looking at the infection.

"How long has he been like this?" she demanded. "Why hasn't this wound been treated in the usual way?" As she fired these questions and many more, she didn't give the nurse the opportunity to reply. I thought once again that she was the worst kind of bully. "Who is the doctor in charge here?"

I approached and told her firmly that I was in charge and she had no business interfering. It was as if I had lit a fuse.

"Well, you need to do your job properly. His leg is badly infected and needs urgent attention."

I told her that I was treating this man and her opinion was neither helpful nor professional, so would she please step aside and worry about her own patients? The ensuing row was heard across not just the ward, but the whole floor and perhaps the rest of the hospital as well. A hundred faces – patients, nurses and doctors – were looking our way. Finally, Dr Jenny stormed out, but not before getting the last word in, stating in her crisp Scottish brogue that my work should be examined by a panel of doctors to consider my competency.

It had been a terrible row and I hated the awkward situation. I am a quiet person and loathe displaying too much emotion, which often causes both sides to say things they regret afterwards. Disagreements between professional staff should be conducted in private.

As I finished my work and walked across the ward and down the corridors, I could hear chatter stop when I passed, see the guilty looks of my colleagues. I felt humiliated and furious. To make matters worse, she could have been right: out of concern for his mental wellbeing, I hadn't taken swift enough action in treating the young Lance Corporal physically.

After this, I avoided Dr Jenny as much as I could, but it was difficult in our close working environment. It was inevitable that our paths would cross again eventually.

CHAPTER 4

From Malta to London

On sunny days, we doctors usually took our mid-morning break in the hospital garden with a welcome cup of tea. We sat on benches and tables, and as I'd found out to my cost, it wasn't good form to talk shop.

As I joined my colleagues the morning after my monster round of drinks, I saw that the odious Captain Douglas was holding court with three male doctors. Today, his subject was women.

"I was involved in training them and I can assure you that male doctors and surgeons are superior in every way. We have better brains and are certainly more skilful with the knife. I can give you several examples: I remember once when I was teaching in London..."

Sitting at a nearby bench, I saw Dr Jenny come into view, and by the look on her face, I knew she had heard Douglas's distasteful comments. She gave him a stare which looked like it was forged in steel.

"Captain Douglas! Not only are your views vile and despicable, but you are prejudiced, bigoted, ignorant, unpleasant and uninformed. You are also completely wrong. Obviously, it would be pointless for me to conduct a logical argument with you – you are far too stupid – and so I am inviting you to a challenge. You and I will attend a medical quiz set by our male and female peers, and afterwards we will perform separate but similar operations, the quality of our work also judged by our peers. The loser will give an apology speech to all of us at dinner, and then resign with immediate effect."

Quietly I applauded Jenny for a masterful performance, so much so I could have walked up and hugged her. I was so impressed with her clever riposte. Douglas stood up unsteadily, his face at first red with fury, and then pale with cold fear. His jaw and lips moved, but no sound came out. I had never seen a reaction like this from anyone before; it seemed to me that he was terrified of taking the challenge and had no idea how to get out of the situation he had found himself in. He tried again to speak, failed, and then stumbled away towards the hospital. It was the best example I had ever seen of someone leaving with their tail between their legs.

Two of the male doctors followed him quietly, not looking at Jenny or anyone else. The rest of us, about a dozen men and women, stood and applauded her. Jenny was overcome as she thanked us. And then we all went back to work.

Our relationship improved after that and we had several conversations at work and during our breaks. I grew very fond of Jenny, particularly when she apologised to me for her earlier brusque manner.

"It was rude and uncalled for and I'm very sorry. I've never behaved like this before and I've spent hours considering my temper and reaction. All I can say in my defence is that to survive, we lady doctors have to work twice as hard as men to gain the respect we deserve. You have no idea of the prejudice I've had to put up with, especially from the male doctors who were training me. Most were horrible bullies who fundamentally believed that women were inferior to them. The older ones were outraged that we should even imagine that we could be doctors, and certainly we could never be as good as them. I really hope you can begin to understand what we have to go through."

She smiled wryly, then continued:

"I've agonised about my appalling behaviour to you and I can't understand why I lost my temper in such a deplorable way. I can only think that we take our frustration out on the ones we care for, and I was under huge pressure at the time."

I was stunned to hear her saying this, and for a moment the world felt a bit unreal.

"We humans are strange creatures and we often behave in ways that make no sense at all. Henry, I'm sorry. If there's anything I can do to make up for my behaviour, please tell me. I should have kept all my abuse for that awful, despicable Douglas – what has happened to him, by the way?"

I realised that we had reached a significant moment in our relationship. I managed to reply in a steady voice, but with great difficulty.

"He has disappeared. It's rumoured that he applied for a transfer to another hospital, and even tried to get a passage back to England, so he must have been able to persuade our seniors to remove him. Anyway, good riddance to him. I never liked him with his air of supremacy and his sneering attitude to those he wrongly believed to be beneath him. I hope those who listened to him and sometimes agreed with him are now feeling remorse and shame. One or two of them do seem a little sheepish."

"I have had three nurses complain to me about his lewd behaviour towards them," Jenny said. "I was horrified and repeated their words to the Colonel. Of course, he did nothing about this, which I believe is scandalous. I was going to challenge him about his inaction, but it would seem I'm too late." She looked me in the eye, then continued, "Henry, you are a good doctor with some great skills. Our abilities and training are very different, but together, we would be an excellent combination. What do you think?"

That was the first time Jenny suggested the idea of us going into any kind of partnership. When I'd managed to overcome my amazement, I realised it was a very good suggestion – as all her suggestions tended to be, even if she did sometimes voice them a little forcefully!

With the demand for our services ever increasing, our opportunities to meet up privately were rare and extremely precious, but as the months went on, we developed deep bonds and talked more about our future. Jenny had originally planned to return to Edinburgh, working in hospitals where her services were desperately needed, but while I would follow her wherever she wanted to go, my strong preference was to work in St Thomas's Hospital in Lambeth. Fair minded as ever, Jenny soon came around to my way of thinking. London would be more practical for us; we were now so close that separation after the war was over was not an option, and the opportunities for learning and development in England's capital were too tempting.

With our plans to move to London set, I wrote to St Thomas's Hospital, in particular to an old Dublin colleague who was now working there, asking about likely vacancies. I also asked my friend if he knew of any landlords who might accommodate two youngish doctors.

As soon as we received positive news from the hospital, Jenny wrote to her father, a Christian minister, who replied saying he would be delighted to perform our wedding ceremony – of course, we could hardly move into rooms together until we were married. All our plans eventually came to fruition when we were joined together at the Canongate Kirk in Edinburgh just days before we were due to start at St Thomas's.

After the wedding service, we took the train back down to London and moved into our new digs just a mile from the hospital, offering us a refreshing walk to and from work each day. The work was hard and the days long, but we settled in well, and when we had time, we took the opportunity to use the extensive hospital library and learn from colleagues. I was able to do more research into my specialities and Jenny developed new surgery techniques.

A Chinese doctor had been invited to St Thomas's Hospital to introduce the ancient practice of acupuncture, a new concept in the United Kingdom at the time. Jenny went to the first lecture he gave, and thereafter attended several practical demonstrations on volunteers, who were mostly wounded veterans of the war. The treatment eased pains, but despite the fact it was rumoured to ease the symptoms of shell shock, too, I decided not to study acupuncture with her. I was already busy with other work and projects, so we agreed to develop separate skills to work more effectively as a team in the future. If I'm to be brutally honest, I didn't have as much faith in the practice as Jenny did; I thought that some of the results were disappointing.

It was usually dark by the time we made our way home and we took the opportunity on our walk back to our digs to talk, mainly about our hopes and plans for the future. Jenny spoke of her dream of buying our own medical practice where we could both look after local people. She was keen to charge people according to their means rather than excluding the poor; we both believed that all people deserved good and equal medical care. We wanted to work and live in South London, so we decided to search for suitable premises.

After long and extensive enquiries, we found a large house in Herne Hill which was ideal for our needs. We had no idea how to go about raising the huge amount of money required to buy this house, knowing nothing about finance and mortgages, so a colleague advised us to visit a bank manager. We will never forget our first meeting with this most arrogant man. He was balding and overweight, and Jenny wasn't slow to give him some health advice.

Perhaps that wasn't the best way to go about asking for a business loan.

"But you see, my dear," he had an enormously annoying habit of starting each sentence the same way as he spoke to Jenny, "that's an awful lot of money. You have only just started work and you are looking to borrow seven hundred and fifty pounds? What kind of collateral do you have? I think you should give up and go back to work for a few years and save as much as you can. This bank can't help you."

I was furious and disappointed in equal measures, and I could feel waves of frustration emanating from Jenny beside me. Before she could come out with one of her trademark caustic comments, I blurted out the first thing that came into my mind.

"You remind me of a Captain we used to work with in Malta during the war."

The man raised his eyebrows, a sardonic smile on his face, and we knew the meeting was at an end. However, we didn't take his advice and contacted as many banks as we could, and when we were able to, we took time off for appointments – we had to attend many singly. I took along copies of our certificates to strengthen our case and prove that we were capable of creating a successful practice, but after months of appointments and form filling, we had been rejected by every bank we had approached.

On our regular walk home, I suggested we change tack.

"Perhaps we should leave it for a couple of years until we are more settled and have a better track record," I ventured.

"Nonsense! This is one of many challenges we are going to face, and if we give up now, it doesn't bode well for the future. We should speak to as many people as we can to get ideas and find opportunities."

Jenny was not the type to give up easily, but I really had no confidence that we could get the mortgage we needed. This was likely to be the pattern of our future and we would have many more challenges to face.

But in the end, the solution to our current dilemma came from a most unexpected source. After several months of trying to raise the capital we needed, I received a call at the hospital. To my amazement, 'Captain Douglas', as we had nicknamed the arrogant manager of the first bank we had visited, was on the other end of the line. He asked us to call in as soon as possible.

A slimmer and fitter version of 'Captain Douglas' greeted us as we were ushered into his office.

Perhaps Jenny's words had had a positive effect on him after all.

"Well you see, my dear, we have started a new scheme at the bank: we are looking more favourably at those who were active abroad during the war years, especially those who performed Christian acts saving the lives of other people. The bank has given me the authority to make decisions on its behalf, but I will need as much evidence as possible of your actions. Do you think you could get some references together in the next couple of weeks?"

Of course we could! I copied certificates of our service in Salonika and Malta and asked several colleagues for honest references. Dr Edmund, who had become a good friend, testified to my actions in saving the life of Tom Haslam, the wounded soldier who had become trapped in barbed wire, and others vouched for our medical work. I revisited 'Captain Douglas' two weeks later and presented the evidence to him. He asked me to phone him in a week's time.

"Well you see, old chum," he said when I called – at least he didn't call me 'my dear', "I've given your case a great deal of thought and have decided to give you the mortgage."

I was standing in the hallway of our digs and had to find a chair to sit down on, quickly. Dizzy and breathless with excitement, I couldn't wait to tell Jenny. But 'Captain Douglas' hadn't finished speaking yet.

"Just one more thing, Dr Smythson: on our first meeting, you compared me to a Captain you once worked with in Malta. I would be interested to know why…"

Part Two

Isla

CHAPTER 5

Pins and Needles

I felt the pins as she pushed them one by one into the skin of my stomach. The pain wasn't too bad, but the process made me nervous and I winced and quivered as she carried out her mysterious work. I looked at her face and saw the lines of fierce concentration as she kept going, seeming to know instinctively where each pin should go.

Her round spectacles had slipped to the end of her crooked nose, but she did not adjust them. Her pupils moved closer together for greater concentration, but this just made her look like the cross-eyed clown in the park and I almost laughed out loud. But this would have brought a stiff rebuke from her. I dared not move.

I looked down, seeing twelve tall pins sticking upright in an apparently random pattern, and slowly the dreadful pain inside my stomach eased a bit. It had started two days ago and I had not slept since, feeling sick and tired, crying tears of agony and frustration. I did not know what was wrong, and if my mother did, she wasn't sharing the information with me.

She twisted each needle one by one, and then started all over again. She was so focused on her task that it seemed she was ignoring me; if I complained or moaned, I would be wasting my breath. Indeed, if she did respond, it would be with a slap or admonishment.

She twisted one needle a bit too much and I jumped at the sharp pain.

"Honestly, Isla, you have no pain threshold at all. You've no idea what life was like in my day: we dared not complain, but you sniffle and moan at the smallest thing. I really don't know what will become of you. You'll never amount to anything, you know, until you start to show a bit of backbone. Now be still and stop fidgeting!"

I was ready for the next comment:

"You never use that brain which God gave you. You hardly try at school and we work so hard to educate you. I often wonder what will become of you."

My mother had a strong Edinburgh burr, which she'd never lost throughout her years in London, and she often used her accent to emphasise her point. Once upon a time, I would cry when she was harsh with me, which often brought on more criticism, but when I got older, I became so used to her comments that I was more able to ignore them. They still stung me, but perhaps just a little bit less. Once again, though, here she was, making me feel inferior and worthless compared to her.

Mother was such a brilliant doctor and surgeon, she was held in very high regard by all her patients and was in huge demand at St Thomas's Hospital. Even my lovely father, who was similarly qualified, was in awe of her. He was standing quietly by the bookcase in the corner of the room, careful not to interrupt the proceedings. But when my mother berated me, he couldn't remain quiet.

"Oh, Jenny, the poor girl is suffering enough. I am sure Isla will be talented at whatever she wants to achieve. Do leave her alone for a bit."

"She's got to learn," Mother replied abruptly, "or she'll never get anywhere in life. You really should get a grip on yourself, Isla."

I was so pleased to have my father's support. In his double-breasted suit and highly polished black shoes, the only indication that he had finished work being that he had removed his collar stud and opened the top button of his white shirt, he looked so smart. The round pince-nez glasses he always wore, gripping the bridge of his nose to stay in place, gave him an earnest and intellectual look that instilled confidence in his patients as he delivered his diagnoses and advice. He had been bald for as long as I could remember, but this just added to his distinguished air, making him look older than his years. He had a wonderfully soft, deep Irish brogue and never raised his voice. But when he spoke, others in the room would be quiet and listen carefully. I loved and worshipped this good man.

Behind him was the mahogany Victorian furniture which to me always looked dark and oppressive. I disliked the aspidistra sitting alongside a dusty cabinet, making the room look so out of date, and the stiff upright piano. A music teacher came to the house once a fortnight to teach me chords and basic tunes, but I wasn't very musical, unfortunately. Of course, Mother had something to say about it.

"Isla, is there anything you are good at?" Followed by, "If only you would stick to one thing and become competent in that."

I had disappointed her once again.

My name is Isla and I am the only child of Doctors Jenny and Henry Smythson. I was born in 1921 in their large house in Herne Hill, London, which doubled as their medical practice. As a child, I had several bouts of ill health and suffered frequent stomach pains, and I became Mother's guinea pig as she practised her newfound skill of acupuncture.

My parents could not have been more different. Henry, my father, came from a large family in rural Ireland: he, his mother and eleven brothers and sisters had all lived in a small house supported by their policeman father. Henry went on to train in hospitals in Dublin and become an outstanding student at the Royal College of Surgeons. It was a bit of a mystery how his education had been financed, but however it was done, it was a good investment.

Father was so full of love and care for others, and I always marvelled at how clever he was with animals – all animals, but especially our terrier, Pip. He could persuade Pip to walk towards him on his hind legs, turn around and walk back again, the dog earning a small biscuit for his performance. Father had a magical effect on other people's dogs, too, and even their more aloof cats warmed to him. I had decided that I would care for animals in some way during my life and I am sure I inherited this from him.

Father's care was extended to his patients and they loved him in return. They would hang on to his every word and nearly always take his considered advice. He almost mesmerised them and they rarely disobeyed his soft orders or gentle suggestions, especially when he gave them prescriptions for a bottle of Guinness. He fervently believed in its health-giving properties, particularly for pregnant women, but would only allow one bottle a day as he frowned upon drinking alcohol to excess. He deplored smoking of all sorts, believing that this practice was deleterious to one's health (he loved unusual words like deleterious, but fortunately, we had a good *Oxford English Dictionary* in our library).

I loved my father dearly and, in my eyes, he could do no wrong, but I felt sorry for him at times. He showed incredible patience in dealing with my headstrong and opinionated mother, Jenny. The rows they had on an almost daily basis could be fearsome; she believed she was far cleverer than her husband, though this was not true. He was of a much softer character, until he'd had enough of her lecturing when his temper would explode, although he never let his frustration become physical. At this point, Mother's Edinburgh inflection would broaden until her words became incomprehensible.

Mother absolutely terrified me, but I could never be frightened of my father. He was like a pussy cat to me. The only thing the two of them had in common was their passion for medicine – otherwise, they were as different as whisky and Guinness!

"Hold still!" Mother's sharp voice brought me back to the present and I squirmed as she twisted the needles once again. I didn't really understand what was going on, but she had told me that the pins would ease my pain and cure my condition.

The Chinese had practised acupuncture for thousands of years and a doctor had brought his skills from his country to the UK shortly after World War I. Always one to embrace new ideas, Mother had become one of the early practitioners in this country. The Chinese doctor had claimed that the main benefit of acupuncture is pain relief, although Mother practised it for other ailments as well. She believed it eased and helped to cure muscular and joint issues, and many other illnesses.

One day a week, both my parents worked at St Thomas's Hospital, and this is where Mother had first learned about acupuncture from the specialist from China. She told me that the procedure interested her because it benefited the mind as well as the body; she was fascinated by the power of the mind and how it could be used to repair the body. According to her, each treatment could be tailored to the individual to repair mind, body and spirit. She stated that modern doctors knew little about acupuncture and its potential, and she was determined to spread this new knowledge amongst her peers. Father never said what he thought about this practice; he knew better than to voice his opinions.

Apparently, there are twelve main channels in the body through which energy flows – the Chinese call them meridians. These control the main organs of the body, and so can be used to treat and cure a variety of ailments, including my painful stomach problem. Mother was convinced that a patient's positive attitude was more likely to bring about a cure than all the best medicines, hence her constant berating of me if I so much as hinted at a complaint.

She was extremely intuitive. Father used to tell me that she particularly enjoyed her weekly visit to St Thomas's, where she would walk up to each ward via the staircase rather than taking the lift. She claimed that this was good exercise for her and gave her the time to focus on the next few patients she was due to visit, consider their symptoms and work out her approach and prognosis. A well-built woman, she believed the effort it took her to climb the stairs toned her body and clarified her thoughts. She would then be ready to astound her first patient.

"How long have you had kidney stones?" she'd ask, or "When did your heart condition first develop?" or, "Do you realise you are only here because you are drinking too much? Its time you stopped!"

Her patients were always staggered by her outbursts, and the fact she was invariably right. But her forthright opinions could be embarrassing. On the rare occasions when we all went out for lunch or dinner, she would look around the room and fix her stare on one person.

"My goodness – look at his high colour," she'd announce clearly for all to hear. "It's obvious he drinks too much, and I'll bet he smokes, too. He should stop those nasty habits at once! He has already given himself high blood pressure."

I never heard anyone challenge her, so presumably she was always right, and they knew it. The poor individual would look downcast and embarrassed that someone could see inside his or her mind and soul.

I remember her most embarrassing moment came in a crowded café on a Sunday afternoon.

"Look at that huge nose!" she exclaimed, staring at a large woman at an adjacent table. "How unfortunate to be born with a nose like that. How on earth does she drink her sherry? Her nose wouldn't fit inside the glass!"

Sherry was the only alcoholic drink Mother consumed, and she particularly liked Bristol Cream, but I never saw her drink more than two. And the irony of her outburst on this particular day was that *she* had difficulty drinking out of narrow sherry glasses as she too had a large nose!

My parents both travelled to the hospital together in Father's magnificent new Humber Tourer, the journey taking about twenty minutes. He was so proud of that car; back in the thirties, there were very few cars on the road, and none as elegant as his. I loved this car with its sky-blue panels and big black mud guards; its shiny chrome headlights and radiator. Father kept his prized possession in immaculate condition by paying a man to come around once a week to wash and polish it. The car always looked beautiful after his efforts, but Father was never quite satisfied with the results.

One of my earliest memories is of being driven by him up a nearby hill. He hoped to pass a neighbour or patient, stop to offer them a lift, and then show off the car's capacity to climb the hill from a stationary position. Many cars could not do that, so he loved to show off his special vehicle's abilities, although he was normally a modest man.

I also remember him driving me to the Oval cricket ground in Kennington and taking me to watch test cricket there. We always had the best seats as he was the club's doctor when these matches were being played; although I don't remember him ever needing to treat anyone, we didn't even have to pay to go into the ground. I clearly remember watching England playing a visiting Australian side, but can't remember who won on that occasion. Anyway, we only watched one day of that match. I probably only went with him on a couple of occasions, but these days out at the Oval were our special times together; Mother had no interest at all in the game of cricket and never accompanied him.

It always amazed me that my mother never learned to drive. She could carry out complex operations on people, manage modern medical machinery and had a brilliant mind, but driving a car was quite beyond her. She had so much trouble coordinating the clutch and the gears; although she could operate them separately competently enough after several months of practice, she could never quite work them together. Father spent hours trying to teach her, and the subsequent arguments were some of the worst I had ever witnessed. Eventually – thankfully – they both gave up and she never tried again.

CHAPTER 6

Edinburgh

After they were married in 1918, my parents bought a practice in Herne Hill, and this building was also our home. The practice was quite small and they worked with just one nurse.

Just after I was born, they bought another practice in Coldharbour Lane in nearby Camberwell. This was much larger and they were able to employ half a dozen general practitioners. They were extraordinarily successful in business and we lived a good and prosperous life, although most of the time, they were both working extremely hard over long hours.

Mother had been one of the first female doctors to qualify in Edinburgh. The daughter of a severe Presbyterian pastor, the Rev AK Walter, she had learnt to read and write ancient Greek by the age of four. She excelled at school, and then studied medicine at the Edinburgh Medical College for Women to become one of the finest doctors of her generation. An avid proponent of equality, she actively supported the Suffragette movement to promote more women in medicine.

On one of the rare occasions my parents took a holiday, we travelled as a family on the train from London to Edinburgh and stayed with my grandfather in his cold sandstone house, which matched his personality almost perfectly. Not yet in my teens, I didn't like him at all, and I was so pleased he was not my father. For some reason, all I remember eating while we were there was a rather foul-tasting soup that he claimed was called cock-a-leekie.

The day after we arrived in Edinburgh, we went for a long walk, my parents and I, through the streets and narrow alleys so that Mother could show us her home city. I walked between the two of them, holding my father's hand while Mother's pride and enthusiasm shone through as she took us along her memory lane. She showed me the streets she used to march down proudly as a member of the Suffragette movement, waving flags and banners in purple for loyalty and dignity, green for hope and white for purity.

"We used to carry a banner showing a snake entwined around a pole, known as the Caduceus. This has been the emblem of the medical profession since the days of ancient Greece," she told us. Father knew all of this, of course, but was wisely keeping very quiet.

Mother admitted that some of the Suffragettes had thrown stones and broken windows in government buildings, but of course, she had not. Some of her friends were even locked up, suffering terrible deprivation or the pain and indignity of being force fed. Mother told me that Suffragette women would do almost anything to force the government and society to give them the vote.

"Some of my colleagues bombed Edinburgh's Royal Observatory, you know. I didn't believe that we should be violent, but a certain element did. The authorities never knew for sure who was involved, and I would never tell. That was the year before I qualified."

I loved the city of Edinburgh; I doubt if there is a more beautiful city on God's earth. We weren't far away from the iconic castle and soaring crags, the historical sites and famous institutional buildings. I felt very important, walking along the elegant streets as trams and box-like cars glided past, wearing my new pink woollen coat. For once, I had persuaded my mother to buy me something modern and nice. Gosh, I was so smart. I really wished my school friends could see me now as I walked with a smirk and swagger.

"Och, it's a dreich day," Mother stated as we made our way through the streets. The word didn't need translation; the day was dreary and bleak with the threat of early darkness and rain. Father and I looked at each other with a knowing wink.

Matrons bustled by in their long dresses and colourful bonnets; men in trilby hats and tweed jackets added elegance as they strode confidently past. Mother was wearing her long fur coat, advertising her position among the wealthy women of the time.

Father explained that Edinburgh was a city of lawyers and bankers, while Glasgow contained the factories and warehouses of the Industrial Revolution. Massive, elegant granite buildings graced the sides of the long streets, crowned by the huge square block of the world-famous Caledonian Hotel. Mother pointed out Jenner's Department Store and showed me the Caryatids: the pairs of sculptured female figures serving as columns supporting the building above them. I asked her what they were for and she explained that they depicted women as the supporters of the home; she didn't sound very impressed as she fervently believed that women were much cleverer than men and were able to work to a higher standard.

Mother showed us the Edinburgh Medical College for Women where she'd trained, winning the Dorothy Gilfillan Memorial prize for being the most distinguished student of her class. For this, she was awarded the sum of thirteen pounds. The training had taken five years to complete and she said it was the toughest time of her life. She and her fellow students were trained by male doctors, most of whom were rude and patronising.

"We didn't have the strength to become surgeons, according to them, but we might just be capable of giving anaesthetics. You can imagine my response when I heard these ridiculous comments, although actually, it's quite a difficult procedure using chloroform. Applying too little is more dangerous than giving too much. I preferred using the Shipway masks using chloroform as well as ether, but I am drifting from the point.

"Emmeline Pankhurst, the leader of the Suffragette movement, had said that the decision to become a doctor was an exceedingly difficult choice for a woman. You've got to realise, Isla, that only a few years back, women were regarded as second-class citizens and had never had the vote. Against this prejudice, I managed to become a Bachelor of Medicine and a Bachelor of Surgery."

"How can you be a Bachelor if you are married?" I asked.

"Now, don't be facetious, Isla!"

I wished I hadn't made that idiotic comment as this was the first time my mother had spoken so openly to me and I was happy to be treated as a grown up for once. She wasn't talking down to me like she usually did and I loved hearing all about her early life. I could believe that she had achieved so much in such difficult circumstances, she was that impressive.

"The hours we students worked were long and arduous," she told us, "and we were pale-faced with exhaustion. One of my peers took her own life with drugs she had taken from the medical cupboard."

Oh my goodness! It all sounded horrible and the Edinburgh Medical College for Women was grim and dirty. I have to admit, I had not appreciated what she'd had to go through to qualify and gain her subsequent awards.

Mother took us to the Craiglockhart Poor House where she'd worked after qualifying. The building was pleasantly designed and much larger than I'd imagined; I felt so sad for the people who were forced to live there, but at least they received free healthcare and food, although the fare sounded appalling. The sexes were separated and had to work for their shelter and care.

"I was the Resident Medical Officer here after a short spell at the York Dispensary. As lady doctors, we were only allowed to work in places like poorhouses. We were seriously understaffed, but our contribution helped to improve the lives of the people in the poorhouse, and some went on to become independent citizens, bringing up their own families and holding down regular jobs."

Mother went on to say that this was one of the best jobs she had ever had as the people she treated were so grateful for even the smallest touches of care she gave. She believed her contribution in the poorhouse mattered hugely as she and many others worked hard to improve people's lives.

I had never heard her talk like this before and her words had a great effect on me; I would remember them for the rest of my life. When I look back, I thank goodness for the National Health Service we have in the UK today.

Father took us for afternoon tea in the magnificent Caledonian Hotel. I don't think I had ever been in such a huge and elegant place in all my life. We were ushered towards our table in the centre of the room by a man in a smart suit with striped trousers. He looked very old and held his nose in the air, which made him look rather silly.

I remember lots of crisp white linen and shiny silverware. The china came in pretty colours and patterns, but the best spectacle of all was the massive black grand piano in the centre of the room which had been polished so much, it must have worn some of the wood away. A young man was rolling his fingers along the white and black keys, producing sounds like running water on a warm summer's day.

I was given a glass of milk, which I loathed, but I knew better than to complain. I wasn't too worried when the waiters served us a tiered stand of delicious sandwiches and creamy, jammy cakes.

As we ate, Mother took the opportunity to share more information about her years of training to be a doctor. She described the terror of the post-mortems where the women didn't dare flinch in front of the male doctors who were watching for any sign of weakness. She listed a huge range of course subjects including vaccinations, pathology, therapeutics, clinical surgery, mental diseases and the history of pharmacy. Father listened intently and compared notes with her on his own college experiences.

"My speciality at college was the study of venereal diseases and dermatology," he stated. "I was one of the first doctors to use Salvarsan to cure syphilis."

"Henry! Not in front of Isla!"

My mother clearly knew all about his speciality, but I hadn't a clue what he was talking about. It all sounded very unpleasant.

To change the subject, Mother cast her eagle eyes around the room, scanning the many customers seated at adjacent tables, her little round spectacles balanced on the end of her nose, her hair scraped back and tied in a bun. Her appearance never varied.

"Look at that man over there – the skinny one with his eyes too close together. Yes, that one." She enunciated every single word, projecting them to all parts of the room as if she were a trained actor. Father and I shrank down in our seats in acute embarrassment. The waiters stopped moving and stood like statues. I desperately wished to be anywhere else in the world but here. "I can never trust a man whose eyes are too close together. It's a shame he has kidney issues..."

"Mother, don't say another word!" I shouted. All eyes in the room were on us; I was so ashamed. Fortunately, for once, she shut up immediately.

The next day, my lovely father took me to Edinburgh Zoo while Mother stayed with the Austere Rector, as I'd named my grandfather. They probably took the opportunity to practise their irregular Greek verbs together, while I was enjoying being fascinated by the seals. Their keeper threw fish for them, which they never failed to catch and swallow whole. In between each tasty treat, they croaked and rasped for more.

I also loved the penguins, lined up like ranks of soldiers and wobbling forward while swaying from side to side. They were really funny, just like Charlie Chaplin in the lovely black and white films we saw at our local flea pit. And then the elephants – I couldn't believe how big they were.

However, my favourite animals were the two Koala bears who were playing together like cuddly children. I adored them and wanted one to take home – I wanted one so badly that I cried that night, then begged my sweet father to get me one. He did agree to ask an explorer friend who had cared for the bears in Australia, but the man explained that he wouldn't be allowed under any circumstances to send a Koala bear halfway around the world for me to keep as a pet. I can't remember ever being so disappointed before or since. Oh yes, actually, I can. It's just come to me: I made my father promise to visit me after he died, but he never did.

I had never been to the zoo before. The day turned out to be one of the best of my life, and spending it with my father was the cream on my cake. I decided then that when I had children, I would take them to the zoo at every opportunity.

To my joy, my mother continued to open up to me during our stay in her home city. I listened, fascinated as she explained how she'd become involved in treating the wounded of World War I.

"I received a letter from a senior lady surgeon asking if I would serve with the Royal Army Medical

Corps abroad. All lady doctors received the same letter, explaining that we would be civilians and would not have a military rank, unlike our male colleagues. I was annoyed at this unfairness, but was used to it by now and immediately responded by saying yes, I would be delighted to be included. There were eighty of us who volunteered, and over the next few months we travelled to Malta and Salonika to carry out our work."

"When did you get this letter?" I asked.

"It must have been early in 1916 and I travelled to Malta in September that year."

"I was posted there the year before," Father added, "but unlike your mother, I had joined the RAMC and had the rank of Captain."

"You men had all the privileges, unlike us poor women who were, in fact, much better trained." Like many professional women, Mother took every opportunity to remind the male population of their 'inferior status'. "I travelled on HMHS *Essequibo* – that's a hospital ship – in September 1916, together with seven other women doctors. The ship was terribly crowded and we weren't surprised that no special arrangements had been made for us on board. However, we had faced much worse in our careers, and at least our male colleagues on board were polite to us."

"How much were you paid? And did you have a uniform?" I asked.

"We were contracted to work for twelve months for twenty-four shillings a day, which was quite good pay in those days, and we were told that if we were good girls and didn't get into any trouble, we would receive a bonus of sixty pounds at the end of our contracts. It must have been a male who decided that! Unlike the men, we weren't given a uniform – at least, not at first."

"By the way, where is Salonika?"

"Salonika is in Greece, although over its history, the city has been claimed by many countries. The wounded were transported from Salonika to Malta, which is a journey of around a thousand miles. We had many good hospitals in Malta, but the journey wasn't straightforward and could take several days, particularly if we were avoiding U-boats. They were a real menace and sank several of our hospital ships, often with all on board lost.

"We were sent to Salonika to set up hospitals there. The work was very hard and we became tired, but we were all determined to carry on and do our best. And it was in Salonika that I met your father. We didn't get on at all at first, but that is another story."

"What happened between you?"

"That's private, Isla! You shouldn't ask your parents questions like that."

That simply made me even more determined to find out one day.

CHAPTER 7

The Countdown to War

Back at home, I spent much of my time playing on my own in my bedroom or doing homework. The teachers always gave us piles of work each evening, so I had many hours of solitude and I hated the loneliness of those times. Often the only company I had was our nurse, Kay, and although she was much older than me, she became my confidante. I could trust her with almost anything and she would either just listen and nod, or offer words of advice. I also took great comfort in my dolls and a Pooh Bear I had received as a Christmas present and loved more than most people. Last but not least, I enjoyed playing with Pip, the family dog, but he wasn't allowed upstairs at all.

I determined that one day, when I was free of this imprisonment, I would live independently and go out to the West End with my friends. I looked forward to the day when I would have a caring husband and happy children running around my light and airy house. None of my furniture would be old and dusty, and no aspidistra would ever darken my door. We would have dinner parties and my children would bring their friends home from school to play games: pass the parcel and pin the tail on the donkey. In the meantime, though, I was crushingly bored and lonely.

Our house was large, so we had a cook and cleaner and, of course, Kay. We lived a comfortable life – I had no complaints about that, but my isolation made me miserable. I wore expensive clothes, but my mother usually combined ugly, chunky materials with boring tailoring. My big black block shoes, which she called sensible, were the worst items in my wardrobe; I just hated wearing them. I used to dread leaving the house, especially to go to school, always worrying about the other girls who constantly criticised my clothes. As a result, I was too self-conscious to speak out in class and became rather withdrawn. When the teacher asked me a question directly in front of the others, I would feel my blood rising and cheeks reddening. I often cried when I got home after suffering so much humiliation.

It helped me to feel better if I expressed my thoughts and feelings in a daily diary, and I've kept this practice up all my life – when I finally did become a mother, I recorded almost every moment of my precious babies' early lives. As a child, I would write about my experiences and impressions, making sure I kept my diaries in a secret place as I couldn't bear the thought of anyone else on earth reading them. That would be too awful to contemplate.

I was often embarrassed by the name my parents had given me – Isla – and the girls at school used to tease me about it. They called me Isla Wight and Isla Man, and someone once called me Isla Lesbos, but that barb was wasted on me – I didn't know what they meant. Some of my friends called me Issy – yes, I rather liked that, but when one girl called at our house asking for Issy, she was sent away with a flea in her ear. Mother, of course, telling her that no one lived here with that name. I still cringe as I recall this.

When I was older, I enjoyed school more. I made some good friends at nearby James Allen's Girls' School and I was often invited to their homes, but Mother would never let me bring any of them back to our house. It was even a struggle to get her to agree to me going to theirs; she would say that they were not the 'right sort' or were 'too common'. She embarrassed me terribly and I was generally unhappy as a result.

When I was eleven or twelve, I suffered with a horrible ear infection and spent many months in hospital and nursing homes. I particularly remember a huge draughty building in Bentinck Street near Oxford Street in London. The place was otherwise comfortable and the staff were kind, but the long hours there were lonelier than ever. Every week, my lovely father came to visit me, and I well remember our drives around Hyde Park in his large car. I felt like a glamorous princess being chauffeured to my London palace, but I was still relieved when I was finally allowed to go back home.

During our drives, I had an opportunity to ask Father why he and Mother had come to work in London.

"Even when I was training in Dublin, I wanted to work in London where I could absorb medical books and papers in the hospital libraries. Many of the world's best doctors worked there and there were huge opportunities to rub shoulders with them and increase my own knowledge and skills."

I have clear memories of a significant event at around this time; I would have been in my early teens when I awoke in shock one night to find my bedroom lit up. Looking out of the window, I saw an enormous glow shining brightly in the distance. A huge pall of smoke flowed upwards from the orange centre of the glow and seemed to fill the sky, its sheer size making it appear to be so close to us.

At breakfast the next day, my father announced, "The magnificent Crystal Palace has been destroyed by fire. There is hardly a trace left. This is a very sad day."

We had only visited this landmark the previous week! I remembered admiring the beautiful huge glass structure and couldn't believe there was nothing left of it. It had originally been built in London's Hyde Park by Prince Albert, Queen Victoria's dear husband, and housed the Great Exhibition of 1851, which showed off creations and achievements from many countries. I was saddened by how completely it had been destroyed, but little did I know then how this event would pale into insignificance by the side of the losses London would have to endure when the dark shadow of war was once again cast over the world.

During the long summer holidays, I was often sent to stay with relatives in Ireland. Although my father's family lived modestly, he seemed to have extremely wealthy uncles and cousins. One of them had a big manor house with plenty of land and lived a life of leisure, enjoying country sports. I used to run with the other children, chasing the riders and hounds while they hunted down foxes. Later, I was allowed to ride with them and had my own red coat made to measure. After my first ride, I was exhausted, and while I was lying on the ground to rest, the master of the hunt approached me with the tail of the fox the hounds had just killed, and bloodied my cheek. The whole practice seems rather barbaric now, but at the time it was normal and a proud occasion for me.

In Ireland, every day seemed to be sunny with warm breezes. It probably rained a huge amount, too, but childhood memories often block out the bad days, and I fell in love with this beautiful and magical country. I went walking before breakfast each morning with my aunts and uncles and cousins through a low mist which covered the land most days, and I could imagine fairies and goblins going about their business – not to mention the leprechauns. Everyone loved telling and listening to fairy stories, and I still believe in them all today.

Later in the morning, but still before breakfast, we would let the hunting dogs out and feed them. All the dogs were light in colour, but coming back from a long, hot day's hunting one afternoon, I noticed that one of them was jet black. Assuming my uncle must have acquired a new dog, I thought nothing more about this until we were dining at the long table that evening and the conversation turned to the success of the day's hunting.

It was then that I mentioned the black dog and everyone became deathly silent. My uncle at the head of the table went white with shock and I innocently asked what was wrong. He told me that for many generations past, a black dog appearing in the pack signalled a death in the family.

"I'm afraid that the old lady has just passed away." He rushed upstairs to where his mother had lain for years, sick in bed. Sure enough, when he called down to the rest of us, it was to tell us that she had died. I felt guilty, as if I had caused her death.

On a happier occasion, my uncle called me and the other children into his study, and with great ceremony opened his safe.

"I am about to show you something which I value beyond gold and diamonds," he said gravely, taking out a tiny red boot which he said had been found in the grounds by his great-grandfather. "This", he announced dramatically, "was worn by a leprechaun. Look inside – you can see where his foot has worn away the fabric."

"Ooooh," we all said in unison as he passed it to us for our inspection.

I was to learn much later that this uncle's family had financed Father throughout his medical training. They'd arranged for him to attend the Royal College of Surgeons in Dublin, and to this day, the custodians will show you a full record of the work and research he carried out there.

They were happy days, spent running wild in Ireland. I always felt rather miserable leaving my relatives as the boat took me across the Irish Sea and the train carried me back to my lonely and restricted existence in dismal London. But despite the rumblings of trouble across Europe, little did I know just how much our lives were about to change.

It was 3 September 1939. Mother, Father, Kay and I had grouped around the radio, listening carefully to Prime Minister Neville Chamberlain. I can still hear his dour, exacting tones:

"I am speaking to you from the cabinet room at 10 Downing Street…"

There had been rumours flying around for several years, but the announcement that Britain was officially at war with Germany still came as a bit of a shock. I wondered how it would affect our lives and my future. I didn't know what it really meant and I was concerned for my parents, hoping they wouldn't be sent away for the war effort. Would we be invaded and become part of Germany? Several countries were being attacked and occupied by the Nazis and we believed that the people there were having a terrible time.

Mother, pragmatic as ever, said, "Life must carry on as normally as possible and your education, Isla, is very important and shouldn't be affected just because there is a war on."

I was determined to do my bit to support the war effort when the time came, but things seemed to take many months to get started. I was so worried about the future, I suffered horrible nightmares for a time, but life carried on as normal, just as Mother had said.

Then my moment for freedom finally arrived when Mother ordered me to attend a domestic science college. Despite having been an active Suffragette, fighting for women's rights, she expected me to learn how to look after a house and a husband and bring up a brood of healthy children. Nonetheless, I was really excited about the prospect of getting away from London.

Father drove me to Paddington Station where I met a group of six girls under the main clock before travelling with them to Torquay by train. During the long journey, we never stopped talking about our lives and hopes, and about the war which had just been announced. I got on particularly well with one girl, Eva, and we were to become lifelong friends.

We were met by a member of the college staff at Torquay and were excited to be taken to the same hostel and share a room together. Unfortunately, there was only one bathroom for around twenty girls, but this didn't matter as we were all so thrilled about being away from home for the first time. The hostel was only a short walk away from the college and we eagerly looked forward to gaining new experiences there.

As it happened, many of our lessons were rather boring. I was so pleased to have Eva's company as she made us laugh hysterically and helped the time to pass, her favourite remark being to call the teachers cretins!

I wrote in my diary every day about the different teachers we had. One had spent most of her life in India as a cook for an English family and was very interested to hear that Eva had been born in India after her mother had travelled there on her own during World War I. Another teacher had been a missionary in Africa and had many stories to tell. We joked that the locals tried to put her in a pot for lunch but she wouldn't fit. She was rather large!

Looking back at my diaries recently, I read that I was taught how to iron ten handkerchiefs at once in order to save time. No wonder we found the lessons boring! The teachers showed us how to cook and cost meals, and I read some recipes I had written down: a boiled cod, vegetables and plum pudding lunch for four at a cost of three shillings and threepence halfpenny, working out at approximately ten (old) pence a head. A boiled mutton, vegetables and Spotted Dick lunch for three was just eight pence each – about 3p in today's money. We also learned how to cook for large parties of thirty or more people.

We went down to the local RAF Station and the hungry airmen were delighted to have a dozen young women cooking them lunch. I've heard people say that the way to a man's heart is through his stomach, and it certainly proved true that day as we struck up friendships with the diners. Eva and I were even invited to a dance. Unfortunately, the hostel had strict rules and we were locked in at 10.30 every evening.

"That's such a nuisance. How can we ever get to the dance?" I asked.

Eva always had the answer. "That's no problem. All we need do is tie together our sheets and climb down that old drainpipe."

It worked perfectly and the evening was the best of my life so far. We danced and drank with the boys until the early hours, but then reality hit home – hard. As far as I could tell, we had no return plan.

"Eva, when we get back to the house, how on earth do we get into our bedroom? Surely we can't climb up the drainpipe."

"No problem," she said with a grin. "I have a plan, but it means staying out here for a few more hours. Good job it's warm!"

And that was how Eva and I came to be strolling through the hostel doors the next morning as if we had just been out for a refreshing early stroll.

CHAPTER 8

Driving in the Blitz

It was easy for me to find the house we had been asked to visit: the roof had completely caved in and the walls had largely crumbled. Clouds of dust filled the air and piles of rubble spilled into the street. There were at least ten helmeted men struggling to carry wood, bricks and lumps of plaster out of the way while looking for anyone left inside, alive or dead.

They had already found three people and carried them out of the house, laying them in a row on the pavement. Two had rags covering their faces and the third, a young girl, was whimpering softly as she jerked and quivered. She had one leg missing and the lower half of her body was covered in blood.

My father, Henry, calmly opened the car door and stepped out into the street carrying his leather bag. As he approached her, I saw with great sadness that she was only in her teens – even younger than me, Henry's own daughter. I guessed (correctly, as it turned out) that he had assessed she only had moments to live.

I stayed in the car and watched as he delivered the fatal injection into her arm, and almost immediately her body relaxed. She would be out of pain now. I had seen him repeat this procedure so many times in the last few weeks that I had become almost inured to the terrible tragedies taking place every day and night.

Father was a strong believer in helping people to die if they were in terrible pain or suffering from a terminal condition. It was one of the few things he and my mother agreed on.

"Would you let a dog suffer like this?" they would ask anyone who questioned their actions. "No, of course you wouldn't, and I won't let humans suffer in terrible pain, either."

They had fierce arguments with some of their colleagues about the practice. There were plenty of doctors who claimed that the sanctity of human life prevented them from ending one.

"Rubbish!" Father would reply, as blunt as Mother for once. "How could you be so cruel as to let your fellow humans suffer so?"

"Because the Church leaders say that you should," was the common reply.

"Then those Church leaders are insensitive, asinine inhuman fools! That's not the word of God."

There was usually no further comment after that.

Father had taught me to drive. I'd found the process really difficult, spending hours trying to get the feel of the three pedals, but unlike Mother, I finally mastered it. I loved driving his big, smooth limousine and was never to enjoy driving anything smaller or less luxurious. I was truly spoilt, learning to drive in such a magnificent car, but the skill was essential for me to carry out my vital work while he looked after the wounded and the maimed in the London Blitz.

The blackout made driving him, and sometimes my mother as well, to the bombed sites extremely difficult and challenging. Several times we hit pavements because I couldn't see the obstacles, and there were bricks, plaster and general debris in the streets, but we were only allowed limited lights on our cars and there were almost none in the houses we passed. The street lighting rules only catered for a thin downlight. Father always sat impassively, never panicking or commenting on my driving, always appreciating the complexity of navigating the darkened streets. Sometimes I felt guilty because I caused damage to his pride and joy, but he never complained.

When we had to drive past burning houses, we could often feel the heat on the inside of the car. The fires also caused dust and smoke that we had to get through while finding our way to the houses we'd been asked to attend. Although I knew the streets well, I struggled to see in the dim light and dust, and every day the bombs had wreaked havoc, meaning we regularly had to take detours and usually got lost. Sometimes, I had to swerve to avoid fire engines and ambulances, giving them all the space I could as their crews were doing such valuable and extraordinary work. But then, so were we.

My father saved the lives of hundreds of people lying on the pavements outside their homes, and others inside when their bodies were trapped under fallen timber and masonry. He risked his own life many times, rushing without hesitation into buildings that were close to collapse. He never left a patient alone on those occasions, treating people of all ages from babies to the elderly. In one house, he was only able to save the life of a toddler as all the other residents, presumably the child's relatives, had died. He would stay with patients until an ambulance arrived, sometimes travelling with them in the ambulance to the hospital. I would follow on later and pick him up.

I often try to recall how I felt at the time. I was only twenty years old, not much more than a child myself. I knew what was going on, of course, and understood that Britain and most of Europe were under serious threat from Germany. We all listened to the radio for information and heard news from the people we met in the emergency services. Somehow, I always thought that we would survive and win the struggle, although my optimism was often seriously shaken. Every day, I was horrified at the devastation caused by the bombing and the destruction of the London I had known. I had seen too much death and desolation in my young life.

I started to assist Father when he was treating the injured and I had to learn fast, although he was always patient with me. Torn and wretched bodies with limbs ripped off and guts spilling out were a common sight; I didn't have time to be squeamish or frightened. Father used to say we had a job to do and we just had to get on and do it, but I worried about him all the time. He kept saying that he and his skills were desperately needed in these dark days so he struggled on, but I knew he couldn't keep up with the pressure much longer. We were both getting extremely tired, but his condition was worse than mine; I had the resilience of youth on my side. Even Mother didn't have the strength to keep going and often stayed at home, working at the surgery.

We were on call day and night, and dreaded hearing the terrible sirens indicating that another wave of German bombers was approaching London. Then the booming of the first bombs would blow apart the fabric of our lives, and shortly afterwards the phone would start ringing. However, I was so proud to be helping my parents and the people of London. I had at last moved on and become a responsible adult and would never have to go back to my childhood – yes, I was very pleased about that. No more lonely days in my room. No more rigid rules.

Some good can come out of bad situations, even in desperate times like war.

Today had started like many others: we left the house in the early evening, the failing light making driving difficult as usual, and made our way towards the docks where we would be visiting families camped out in a local school. I had spent hours studying maps so that I could memorise roads and short cuts – I often had to find alternative routes when my first choice was blocked by rubble from bombed houses. I dreaded seeing the uniformed Air Raid Precaution (ARP) warden step out in front of me with a hand held up, palm towards me, telling me that I would have to find an alternative route, unless I could persuade them to let me through.

After a time, I am sure I knew the London roads better than most taxi drivers. Some were in almost complete darkness and my lights had to be dim. Tonight, the only lights I could see were from the hundreds of searchlights, throwing bright beams blazing into the sky, crossing each other's paths as they probed the leaden clouds looking for the enemy bombers. These lights exposed the huge barrage balloons hanging in the sky like big black elephants, and helped me at least a little in navigating the roads.

An ARP warden had explained to me that the wires of the balloons could cut off the wings of a plane, and sometimes had small explosive charges attached to each end that would break away when impacted. The wires would then wrap around a wing and drag the bomber or fighter plane down to earth. The balloons were frequently successful and the German pilots were afraid of getting too close.

The sirens had not started yet and we prepared our senses for their eerie ululation, which had a terrifying effect on our emotions. At the first wail, the ambulances and fire engines raced along the narrow streets, and we followed. Every half mile or so, we passed an ARP post, and when the helmeted wardens saw our doctor's sign on the front screen, I prayed they would let us through. Mostly, they did. There was still debris in the streets from the raid the night before, and with little light to guide me, I struggled once again to avoid the obstacles.

We passed a house which appeared to have been chopped in half, the bed and wardrobe of one upper-floor bedroom hanging out into empty space and the torn wallpaper flapping in the breeze. Bizarrely, this reminded me of a dolls' house I used to play with as a little girl. Trees on the streets and in the parks were stripped bare as most of their bark had been blasted away. As we turned into another street, a foul smell filled the inside of the car. The pavement had been ripped up and a sewer pipe broken open. Later, we had to endure strong whiffs of gas, but we were getting used to such discomforts.

The school was our destination today as my father was going to re-dress the wounds and treat the sicknesses of the unfortunate people crammed in the basement. Having visited the school several times before, we had got to know many of them quite well, and I was looking forward to their happy faces and cheery welcome. Under awful circumstances, they were always cheerful and calm.

Maisie, a grandmother, had worked in Queen Victoria's household as a seamstress. She, her daughter Violette, three grandchildren and the family dog Buster huddled together in their small space in the basement, always so apologetic for bothering us, never complaining. Maisie would entertain us by telling us scandalous stories about the Queen and the naughtier members of her household. Violette used to try to cover the ears of the children, but they were desperate to hear all the gossip. My guess is that they had heard the stories many times before anyway.

One of their elderly uncles played the piano (or the 'Joanna', as they called it) and everyone sang along with enthusiasm and great emotion. I cried every time I heard *Keep the Home Fires Burning* and *It's a Long way to Tipperary*. The children missed their father terribly – he had been killed in a timber factory during a recent raid – so I would bring in bars of chocolate to cheer them up whenever I could.

After an uneventful but difficult journey, Father and I finally arrived at our destination only to find that the school had completely disappeared, leaving a huge hole gaping in the ground. The whole area was lit up by spotlights. There were dozens of wardens and ambulance men milling around the street, but there seemed little for them to do.

I got out of the car and spoke to one of the wardens who told me what had happened. In the early hours of the morning, just a few minutes after a night raid, the school had received a direct hit. A huge parachute bomb had landed, and by the time we arrived, there was nothing left but a massive empty crater. The people inside the school must have heard the all-clear sound and believed they were now safe. No one would have known that a parachute was carrying its ghastly load slowly down towards them.

I stood on the pavement overlooking the devastation and burst into tears. Maisie, Violette, the children, Buster – all of them had been annihilated. No one had survived; there was not even the smallest trace of life in that deep crater. It was all so unfair and tragically unnecessary.

My father came to stand beside me, hugging my shoulder to comfort me, and we lowered our heads in respect for these poor people. I saw moisture welling in his eyes as he said that this should never have happened and that I should not have to witness scenes like this. Days later, the papers reported that seventy people had been killed, but we knew there were many times that number. I now understood what was meant by the saying 'the first casualty when war comes is truth'.

On our night-time outings, Father and I saw hundreds of damaged houses, and once we saw a whole street that had been almost wiped out. The few survivors, now homeless, had been taken to the ill-fated local school for shelter and were soon joined by many others. We visited the school regularly to treat those wounded from earlier raids. The people were crammed into the basement with almost no washing or toilet facilities. It was a disgrace that the government had abandoned them in this way; the wardens told us that they should have been taken out of London and placed into suitable accommodation in the countryside, but the coaches sent to pick them up had gone to Camden Town instead of Canning Town! No one seemed to care about them.

There was a belief that the poorer classes were being ignored and abandoned while the richer classes were being looked after, and we had heard reports that the government's attitude was leading to civil unrest. Father and I saw hundreds of homeless people roaming the streets and entering the Tube stations so that they could be safe and warm below ground. The stations were officially out of bounds, but the frustrated homeless had broken the locks on the gates, such was their desperation. The people we saw looked tired and depressed, and many we spoke to wanted to leave London. They had received terrible punishment nightly for many weeks, through no fault of their own.

I don't think people today can imagine what the inhabitants of London went through during the Blitz, especially those living in and around the dock areas which were heavily bombed. People were hungry, desperately tired and cold, their relatives and children had been killed or seriously injured, and many of them had lost their hearts as well as their homes. The devastation had often cost them their jobs and now they couldn't afford to feed or clothe their families. Thousands were living on the streets.

The dockland areas were targeted by the bombers which visited London night after night. They easily followed the path of the Thames to find the docks which made the blackout arrangements seem rather futile. The bombers came for seventy-six nights in a row at the height of the Blitz.

When Father and I were travelling to the docks, we could often smell burning sugar and oils, and always charred wood, the smoke merely adding another obstacle to the already difficult driving conditions.

Throughout all this devastation, I had another worry on my mind. Some months earlier, my father had complained about chest pains and Mother had examined him. She'd concluded that his heart was weak and she wouldn't let him drive anymore, which was when he came up with the idea that I could act as his chauffeur. Eventually, though, he became too sick to do this work, or indeed any work at all, and he had to stay quietly at home on the strict orders of my mother. He was worn out, both mentally and physically.

No longer needed as a driver and unable to contribute to the work my parents were doing, I was now free to move on with my life. My new adventure in the Women's Royal Naval Service (WRNS, known affectionately as the Wrens) was about to begin.

CHAPTER 9

Leaving Home

For years, I'd desperately wanted to leave home and have my own life, but when the time finally came, a part of me longed to stay to look after my ailing father. One of my friends from school had told me that she was going to become a Wren – a women's only group serving in the Royal Navy – and had been for an interview. This sounded really exciting to me – I had visions of sailing the seas and visiting mystical and sultry foreign shores. I had never been abroad before, apart from my summer visits to Ireland, and despite my fears for my father's health, I was desperate to join up and start a new life.

When war was declared, I was pretty much old enough to leave school. I had done well in my exams and was top of my form for arithmetic, and I enjoyed playing hockey and cricket – yes, the latter was an unusual sport for girls, but my college, Dulwich, was well-known for it. My father had lit the fire of my enthusiasm with our visits to the Oval and he encouraged my game – once I'd even had ambitions to play for the England Women's team, following their progress in Australia and New Zealand. Their Captain, Betty Archdale, was my heroine and I had pictures of her on my bedroom wall (until my mother made me take them down).

Betty had strong family connections to the Suffragettes – Emmeline Pankhurst was her godmother – which elevated her status even higher in my eyes. My mother was a great admirer of the women in this movement, but she still wouldn't let me put Betty's picture back up.

Another heroine of mine was Myrtle Maclagan who scored the first century for the women's team against Australia. What a fantastic achievement! I became quite good with the bat, but probably nowhere near good enough for the national team, although I did score sixty-three once in an innings. Later, as an adult, I would take every opportunity to visit Lords or the Oval to watch matches, and encourage my children to take an interest in the game, too.

I left school shortly after Mr Chamberlain's rather gloomy declaration of war. It was a frightening time and no one had any idea of how the future would evolve. It was quite a while later, after I had attended domestic science college in Torquay and learned to drive Father around the bombed sites, that I heard from the Royal Naval College at Greenwich, and I was ordered to report there at a specified time.

On arrival, I was interviewed by four rather austere uniformed women who questioned me for around forty minutes. It seemed they were quite impressed by the exam results I presented to them as they told me they wanted me to work on special duties. Mother was not the only clever one in the family after all – I felt much better for knowing that.

Some time later, the people who had interviewed me ordered me to attend basic training at Mill Hill for six weeks. Apart from Ireland and Devon, I had never stayed away from home before and I was nervous about sharing my personal space with so many other girls. But at the same time, as I stepped out of my parents' house with my suitcase, I felt a huge sense of exhilaration and freedom. I would never again live at home, obeying my mother's rules; I was now free to live my own life, have my own friends, go to parties and find a boyfriend (preferably one in uniform).

I walked the short distance from Mill Hill East Tube station to the training centre, seeing hundreds of uniformed Wrens. They seemed to be walking in all directions, so I stopped one who directed me to reception. On announcing my arrival, I was shown to a vast dormitory and told to make my bed. Not too much of a problem, I thought, except it was meant literally – I had to construct a double bunk from a pile of metal and wood. I was joined by other new recruits and we had great fun working out the complicated puzzle. Perhaps this was a test for our future career.

We were given makeshift uniforms and taken to the parade ground where we had to march in step for several hours. This was the drill every morning and we all hated it. What was the point of this repetitive nonsense? Later, we would be kitted out in a smart blue double-breasted uniform with brass buttons that we had to keep shiny and a tricorn hat. We were also given a Navy greatcoat and raincoat and, of course, sensible shoes.

There were classroom sessions where we learned about the Navy, the ranks, traditions, jargon and the many procedures. We were all allocated cleaning duties in the dormitories and bathrooms, and fed in a big canteen, but unfortunately the food was awful.

My fondest memory of that time in my life is the friendship of the group of girls I was with. We came from a variety of backgrounds, and yet we all mucked in together. The conditions were awful, but we supported each other well and got through many ordeals. There were no class barriers and we formed strong friendships which would last for many years, some for a lifetime.

After a while, we were wondering what the special duties were that we would be performing. There were many rumours circulating, but none of us could have guessed what we would actually end up doing. Which is probably just as well, given the secret nature of the work.

A group of us were taken by lorry for cipher training at a huge centre at Stanmore, where we were interviewed one by one by a couple of Naval officers who told us of the importance of absolute secrecy. We must not discuss our work with anyone – even those inside the centre. Then we were told to sign a statement which I understood represented the Official Secrets Act.

The importance of secrecy was drummed into us for many weeks and we soon became used to keeping quiet. We were never allowed to talk to anyone about where we worked or what we did – an officer had scared the life out of us by saying that if we did, we would be shot as spies. We were told at the time that we'd have to keep these secrets for the rest of our lives, but many years later, this rule was relaxed, and several people (like me) have been able to write about their experiences.

The work was hard, repetitive and boring, and the long shifts we covered made us very tired. Fortunately, there was no more drill practice, and we were grateful for this. Our dormitory was cold and the food was still awful, but our spirits were high. The teamwork and friendships we forged saw to that.

After a few weeks, I was given leave for four days and went by Tube to visit my parents, who were surprised to see their child transformed into a smart young lady. My father was still unwell, but otherwise little had changed at home. I started crying when I saw him and we hugged each other tightly for several minutes. I knew he would never get back to the way he had been and probably only had a year or two left; it was a terrible shame as he was not an old man.

My mother came into the room and we hugged, but were both rather awkward with each other. I knew then that our relationship would never be close and I was thankful that she wouldn't have any power over me anymore. I cried again when I was due to return to Stanmore. Wondering if I would ever see my lovely father again, I gave him an extra squeeze as I left.

I had enjoyed my short break, but was pleased to return to my friends and work. We operated large machines called Bombes: early computers used to decode German radio signals from land and sea which had been scrambled by their Enigma machines. All our results went to headquarters at Bletchley Park.

I was surprised to be told I was to be sent to Greenwich to take part in officer training. Some of my seniors had decided that I should be promoted, and after a few weeks, I became a Third Officer. I was then sent to Bletchley Park on a temporary basis, the purpose being for me to understand the link between the work I had been doing at Stanmore and the way it was used at Bletchley, and how to improve communications and results between the two.

I was impressed when I was told that I would be living at Woburn Abbey and assumed that I would be a guest of the Lord of the Manor, only to find that we were allocated a huge wing at the back of the house and never saw him. Later, I learnt that Prime Minister Winston Churchill and his cabinet occasionally met in the mews at the back of the house, so we were in illustrious company after all. Unfortunately, the big room at Woburn that I shared with about a dozen other officers was even colder and more draughty than Stanmore's. However, I looked forward to each day, travelling to Bletchley Park and back, and the experience I would gain.

On my return to Stanmore, I was put in charge of a team of girls and some Royal Naval mechanics who kept our Bombes repaired – they broke down frequently and needed constant attention. Sadly, though, I was now an officer and no longer one of the girls, and I found the transition from worker to supervisor challenging. I made the mistake of trying to befriend the girls under my control, but soon found out I would be despised for this, so began to keep myself apart from them. Slowly, I gained their respect.

However, managing others did not come easily to me, and it was probably years before I developed my skills enough to approach competency. Speaking with other officers and comparing notes helped enormously, and we would socialise together on leave and days off when we could. There was always a dance going on somewhere and we were given free tickets to West End shows.

When Winston Churchill came to speak to us at Stanmore, hundreds of Wrens gathered in the huge hall to listen to the great man. He told us that the work we were doing was vital and would enable our country to win the war. These were stirring words that had an electrifying effect on us, and I am sure we all worked harder and complained less afterwards. Our good work paid off, too: it enabled the Air Force to identify and destroy a U-boat that had been patrolling our shipping lanes, thereby saving hundreds of lives. We received much more feedback afterwards and were sure Churchill had arranged for this to happen to keep our morale high.

CHAPTER 10

First Love

My whole world changed the day I met Tam White.

"Our job is to make the Atlantic safe for our shipping so that we can bring in essential supplies to keep our people alive and healthy. The Atlantic Ocean is three thousand miles across, bordered by the European and African coastlines and the vast American continent, and is two thousand fathoms deep. The sea is dangerous, violent and unpredictable.

"We only grow about one third of the food we need; even with our Land Army and the great work they are doing, we are still producing nowhere near enough. We mine our own coal, but we urgently need to bring in oil. Without oil, our Army, Air Force and Navy will stop functioning within a week.

"Also, we must create safe passage for the thousands of United States troops who need to cross the waters to support the war effort in Europe. The problem is that the German U-boats control these seas and have caused the losses of hundreds of our ships and thousands of our people.

"The German secret service B-Dienst had our codes until recently and we have only just changed them. Through our radio messages we have been unknowingly directing U-Boats, often in packs, towards our shipping, and they have been ruling the Atlantic. Our precious British people are now at starvation point and soon we could be forced to capitulate to Hitler. We would be enslaved by the Nazi yoke and our children's first language would be German – unless, of course, we are all eliminated by them.

"The solution? To break the German codes and ciphers so that we can turn the tables on them. This is your job. When you are successful, we can shorten and ultimately win the war. This is how vital your work is. We must succeed. Failure is not an option. "This is how we are going to proceed…"

We were mesmerised by the man who delivered this powerful message, absorbing every word spoken in a soft burr, an accent I couldn't quite identify. Awestruck by the huge responsibilities weighing heavily on our shoulders, we were determined to live up to the challenge.

Lieutenant Commander Tam White worked in Naval Intelligence and had arrived at Bletchley on the day he delivered his inspiring speech. We all immediately realised that he was a special person, and I for one was looking forward to working with him. Perhaps I wasn't the only one as there were many eager young faces gazing at Tam with hero worship in their eyes. He had an almost magical way about him, an easy charm. Leadership skills came naturally to him.

Tam was short, thickset, stocky and tough. I guessed that he was considerably older than we were, somewhere near forty, which to us girls with an average age in the early twenties was positively ancient. His hands and fingers were stubby like the rest of him, but we were to find out that he was adept at intricate mechanical work. He travelled on an old motorbike which he spent much of his spare time repairing; he was an expert at fixing that machine, and ours.

Tam had many years of experience at sea. Having commanded a corvette which was armed and designed to protect the ships carrying essential food and materials to our shores, he must have had some horrendous experiences; we had heard dreadful stories from our other naval colleagues. Many of our men had died in fires and explosions, and those who managed to jump overboard were often burnt and choked by the oil spreading out from the sinking ships. The survival rates were extremely low.

One young Lieutenant had told how he would go down to his cabin after a long watch and be too terrified to sleep, believing that a torpedo would burst through the thin plating of the ship at any moment. I couldn't imagine many worse ways to die than to be trapped in a sinking ship. The constant work and pressure, the terrible cold and the ever-present fear would break men, and some were removed at the end of a voyage for a life in a hospital where they were treated for horrendous mental stress. We could only imagine what would become of them.

Another man told us that his ship had been protecting a convoy, or at least trying to, but out of twenty-one ships that had started out, only eight made it to port. When a ship was torpedoed and sinking, the other ships would stop to rescue the survivors if they could, but this left them sitting targets for the waiting U-boats. Sometimes, the remaining ships were ordered to leave the men struggling to survive in the water and re-join the convoy for their own protection. To be ordered to leave your mates to die in agony must have been a terrible experience.

The U-boats, of course, would never stop to rescue men from ships they had sunk. The German command stated that this would be showing weakness. The strain and terror our brave men had suffered at sea was unimaginable, and we knew that Tam had endured several years of these horrors.

I could have listened to Tam's honeyed voice for hours, and sometimes I found I was so distracted that I was not taking in the meaning of his words. My mind was drifting as I looked into his soft deep-set brown eyes, his steady gaze suggesting the intelligence and empathy within him. His face was tanned and craggy, topped by dark curly hair just beginning to grey at the sides. His eyebrows were so long and curly, they were almost comical; I was dying to take a pair of sharp scissors to them. I loved the way the corners of his eyes crinkled and creased when he smiled. He may have been powerful, but he was extremely gentle and calm in all situations.

Tam seemed to be quite comfortable in his own personality. One of his most impressive traits was his modesty: although he had hundreds of tales to tell, he was always reluctant to be the centre of attention. He was a great listener and used to say that God had given us two ears and one mouth so that we could listen twice as much as we spoke. Always making the person he was with feel more important than anyone else in the room, he rarely talked about himself and his achievements, and certainly never showed off like many others did. He must have been an inspirational captain, loved by his men.

I fell for him in the first minute of our meeting. The experience was like being hit by a massive thunderbolt, as the Italians often describe falling in love so vividly, and I was dizzy with emotion. He was completely different from the White Knight (although at least I had got the name right!) I used to dream of in my childhood, but I had no doubt at all that he was the one for me. The age difference didn't matter a jot, and I hoped it wouldn't worry him if he were to feel as I did. I wondered if he was married or promised to anyone. Oh, how I hoped not.

I didn't dare share my feelings with my fellow Wrens, of course. They might have been harbouring similar thoughts about him, or if all they saw in Tam was an inspirational officer, I didn't want to be the butt of their jokes. I also didn't want him to know how I felt, while at the same time praying that he liked me as well. This had to remain a private matter for the time being, but I never had the slightest doubt about my feelings.

I had imagined the moment I would fall in love many times during my teenage years, but I never thought that it would be so life-changing and devastating. Did this happen to everyone? I wondered. I would have to take some of my closest friends into my confidence to ask them; I couldn't ask my parents. In the meantime, with Tam around, I was happier than I had ever been or could possibly have imagined being.

But now there was work to be done.

We prepared to spend much of the day and night at our tables, determined to crack the fiendishly difficult Enigma codes. Tam was always there to help and encourage us, and when we got a breakthrough, he would be the first to congratulate us. I led a team of six Wrens and I tried to treat them with the same care and consideration as he did. I made sure they got regular breaks as the work was exhausting and draining, and they needed to leave the hut frequently for some fresh air and a cup of tea or meal in the canteen, although the food wasn't usually as good as the hot drink. I made sure I got breaks, too, but less frequently than my team members.

As the work was so stressful and pressurised, I needed to keep my team fit and well. Sometimes I had to ensure that they were provided with a decent diet and I became unpopular with the catering staff as my demands for a better quality of food were frequent.

We would usually clock off mid evening, but if there was an emergency on, we could stay much later, and sometimes we worked all night. At the end of the shift, we would walk outside into the darkness to one of the waiting buses and travel back to our accommodation. This pattern continued for weeks at a time as we struggled to crack the codes.

We were all interested to know why Tam had become involved with Intelligence. During a rare break in the pressure of our work, he took the opportunity to tell us.

"I was an ordinary seaman serving on corvettes, mainly in the Atlantic. Whenever I had some precious leave, one of my hobbies was solving crossword puzzles. The harder they were, the more I enjoyed completing them.

"The toughest in the world is the *Times* crossword; at the beginning, I struggled to fill in even half of the spaces and realised that I needed to extend my general knowledge. Over time, though, I became more and more competent, and in the end, I could finish them.

"As I practised more, I got to the point where I could often finish the *Times* crossword in minutes. My friends noticed me practising my hobby and marvelled at my skills, asking me to show them a clue and then tell them how I solved it. Even when I told them, though, they sometimes couldn't understand how I'd come to the solution.

"After one particularly fraught trip, as we were pulling into Gladstone Dock on the Mersey, the Captain buzzed down to me and asked me to meet him on the bridge. As I arrived and saluted him, he told me that he had received a radio message saying that I was required to report to a London office near Trafalgar Square as soon as I could. I was to take the train to Euston Station and go to an address in Whitehall, and he gave me the name of the commander I was to report to. He ordered me to take a cab from Euston as there wasn't a moment to lose.

"I asked him what this was all about and believed him when he said he didn't know. I was none the wiser when I got to London, and after an hour of questioning by a strange looking man who took snuff constantly and sneezed from time to time, I was even more confused. I was worried that I was in some sort of trouble, but the snuff man – he looked a little like Einstein, actually – kept me in total suspense.

"I was sent to a classroom where three men in dark suits gave me all kinds of written tests – I found out later that I had performed to their satisfaction. I was then given a *Times* crossword and ordered to solve it as quickly as I could, which I did in about twenty minutes – I didn't have the heart to tell them I had done this one before. I guess that my mates had talked about my crossword solving skills and someone from this office had overheard the conversation. Then I was escorted back to the original office and told that I had been selected to work in espionage. I wasn't asked – I was told!

"I asked when I could return to my ship and was told I wouldn't be going back, at least not for the time being. I was ordered to sign the Official Secrets Act and told that if I ever revealed what I had learnt, I would be taken out and shot, which didn't particularly appeal to me. From the next day at 8am, I would be working in the building in Whitehall and I would need to find digs locally. Easier said than done – it was already dark when I left.

"I spent several months working in the office in civilian clothes, and was then sent to work on ships to decode German radio signals and report back – in code, of course – returning to the office periodically. Over the months, I gradually climbed the Naval promotion ladder and became a Lieutenant Commander. I worked independently on ships under the command of the Captain, but I had seniority when it came to the ship's mission."

I'm sure you can imagine our fascination with his story, but I wanted to know more about *him*. Our group was only a part of a much larger team, but Tam commanded huge respect across the whole operation, and as we now knew, he was able to work independently.

Then Tam made an announcement that really stoked the fire in our bellies.

"I am going to capture an Enigma machine and the enemy's code books," he said. "I want you all to be involved in this project, which has been authorised by the top brass."

Brimming with enthusiasm, we brainstormed the project and put forward many ideas on how to steal these items from the enemy. One by one, each idea was considered in detail, and then rejected as being impractical. We worked late into the night on many occasions, but inevitably, we gradually ran out of ideas.

We then asked other groups to put forward ideas and examined these in detail. One of the best ideas was to steal code books from one of the several air-sea rescue boats which the Germans had just started to operate out of Norway.

"The idea is to take a German bomber which we have captured and crash it into the North Sea, allowing the pilot to parachute out of the plane beforehand," Tam explained. "A group of our men dressed in German pilot uniforms will be waiting close to the crash site on a small raft to attract one of the enemy rescue boats, which we believe will be carrying code books. When the boat comes close, the men will climb aboard and seize the code books before the crew have any opportunity of ditching them." The code books were stored in weighted bags so that they could be thrown over the side of the boat into the sea rather than being captured.

It seemed an extraordinary and implausible idea at first, but when we started planning the finer details, we realised that it had a small chance of success and it was worthwhile to proceed. We would not be part of the operating team, but would write and present the plan to the Admiralty, offering some alternative actions.

After a week of planning and preparing the project, Tam took the train to London to present it. We would have no more involvement in its implementation, so would now start to explore other ideas. Later, we heard that the operation had gone ahead, but sadly had ended in failure: the plane had crashed as planned, but no rescue boat came!

Tam came up with a second idea. "We have been observing German weather ships operating in various parts of the north Atlantic, and months' worth of evidence indicates that they are not using Enigma machines. But they have radioed weather information and it's fair to assume they are using code books. I want you all to develop a plan to surprise and capture a boat we have identified near Iceland."

We immediately started to explore how we could seize the ship before the crew had the opportunity to chuck the books over the side. After many hours of work and discussion, we put forward alternative plans to Tam. He considered each one and, after many rejections, settled on what he thought was the most practical.

Tam would go back to sea to lead the project. He would travel on a frigate as the Intelligence Officer, again with authority over the Captain and to draft in other ships as required. The frigate which had been chosen for this work was coming to the end of a two-month refit; the latest weapons and equipment had been installed, including radar, up-to-date ASDIC devices and a new depth charge launcher. Tam's ship would be one of the most well equipped on the Atlantic.

I was terribly worried for this dear man, realising that he would be exposed to great danger and I would miss him dreadfully during his absence. Fortunately, we had an opportunity to share a table in the canteen before he left. He talked about his forthcoming mission and I told him that we would all be praying for him. I don't think he was used to being fussed over like this and his cheeks reddened slightly, but enough for me to notice.

Then I plucked up enough courage to reach out and take his hand under the table. Squeezing it slightly, I smiled at him and he looked up into my eyes, his face crinkling into a warm and grateful response. His huge hand gave mine a gentle squeeze in return. There was no need to add anything, and indeed, there was no time as we both had to get back to work. But what had happened between us was enough for me, enough to know instinctively that he held the same passionate feelings for me as I did for him.

Part Three

Espionage

CHAPTER 11

Cruelty and Terror

My name is Tam White and I was born in the north of Scotland in 1900. From a young age, I had decided I would spend my working life at sea.

By my third voyage, I was settling into my new career well and thoroughly enjoying the work and camaraderie on board ship, even though we had been thrown into the middle of World War I. We were in the Atlantic and our job was to destroy German U-boats to make the seas safe for shipping carrying our armies and supplies. It was dangerous work and we had already lost dozens of ships and many thousands of good men to these deadly submarines.

Most of the men on board were hard-working, cooperative, good human beings, but sometimes junior officers, particularly those who were inexperienced, threw their weight around and made life unnecessarily difficult for us. One such Lieutenant used his position to bully those beneath him. I just saw him as an overgrown schoolboy, but I felt sorry for the men he picked on as he caused real distress for some. I heard one young rating sobbing quietly at night and the reason was clear: the bully picked on him constantly and belittled him at every opportunity. Like all bullies, this Lieutenant tried to gain support from his colleagues, particularly those who displayed similar characteristics. And like all bullies, he was a coward.

Every day, he gave this poor young rating the worst cleaning jobs and extra watch duties, often after his shift was over. Needless to say, the decks were never clean enough, his uniform was never smart enough, and if he ever did make any mistakes, the bully wouldn't hesitate to humiliate him.

The bullying Lieutenant was from a family with a long Naval tradition going back several generations. He was often overheard bragging about how his ancestors had fought with Nelson. His father had arranged for him to join the Navy, even though he was unsuited to this kind of life and career; in reality, he was totally useless at his job. We all hated him – he was arrogant, crude, rude and ignorant, but he held an officer's position and so was almost untouchable.

When we hit bad weather, the poor rating, who was called Ratcliffe, was left outside, cleaning for an unnecessarily long time. When snow and ice hit us and the cold wind would cut through to our bones, regardless of the protection we were wearing, our lives were at risk up on deck. But hours went past and still the bullying Lieutenant didn't give Ratcliffe a break. The poor man had his body hunched up, trying hopelessly to shield himself from the biting cold.

I knew then I had to do something.

Climbing down the stairs and knocking on the Captain's door, I waited for his response. After a good minute, I heard his loud "Enter" and opened the door. The Captain was sitting at a desk full of books and papers, smoking his pipe. He was middle aged with a greying beard and a spreading waistline, testament to the fact that he liked to leave his officers to get on with the job of running the ship and preferred a background role. We didn't really know what kind of person he was as we rarely saw him, so I could only pray that he was fair-minded.

The glass before him was full of rum and I wondered how many he had already drunk. Not too many, I hoped, as I wanted him to have a clear mind to hear my case and judge fairly when I told him about all the suffering the Lieutenant had caused the young rating.

"Ratcliffe can't take much more of this, sir. The Lieutenant has given him hell at every opportunity, and one day Ratcliffe will snap and fight back, and this could have disastrous consequences."

"Do you want to repeat these accusations in front of this officer?" the Captain asked me. Was that a hint of a threat? My heart sank as I knew he was leading me into a trap with no way out.

"I'm not afraid of facing him here, although I don't think this would be a fair way of finding justice," I replied. "I will be in an impossible situation and I'm sure his venom will then be directed at me."

"Shut up! You do know that this man is one of my officers and his distinguished father is not only an admiral, he also happens to be a friend of mine? I will clap you in irons if I hear any more insubordination from you. Now here's a lesson for you: never interfere on behalf of others. Only come to me if you have a problem of your own. This is none of your damned business!"

Dismissed with a wave of his hand, I went back to work, hoping that the Captain would have a quiet word with the Officer, but if he did, it had no apparent effect. The bullying continued, and if anything, it got worse. It seemed as if the Captain had taken the view that these things happen and bullying is part of the general life on board the ship. Best to leave the crew to get on with it and hope life will settle down in the end. I detected no particular hostility from the bullying Officer, so I could only assume that at least the Captain hadn't revealed that I had been to speak to him.

Days later, the bully made Ratcliffe work outside on deck in the worst conditions we'd faced so far. The weather was dangerously cold and exposure, even in thick clothing, could result in death or serious injury. The wind would hit a person like a thousand shards of glass and could cause serious ice burns. Huge waves were breaking over the bow of the ship, forcing it downward until they dispersed, and ice was forming on the deck, thickening with every wave. The extra weight caused the ship to sit dangerously low in the water and the subsequent large waves forced it down even further. Ships had been known to be so heavily weighted with ice that they were unable to ride the waves and sank to the bottom of the ocean.

The bullying officer ordered Ratcliffe to take a spade and break up the ice. When he went to check on Ratcliffe's work, he decided he wasn't working fast or effectively enough, but Ratcliffe was exhausted and his body was giving way in the terrible cold. The waves were hitting him and knocking him over and he was soaking. Each time, he managed to get back on his feet, but the water on his clothes was freezing, forming ice. I prayed that a more senior officer would witness this dreadful mistreatment and take action to stop it.

At last, the bully brought Ratcliffe inside and sent him down to the canteen, probably thinking he would have a death on his hands if he didn't which he would have to explain. I followed Ratcliffe and made him a cup of hot chocolate, seeing immediately that he had reached the limit of his endurance and could take no more. He was crying softly as I helped him to take off his drenched coat and rubbed his arms and back to get his blood flowing and some feeling into his limbs. Two of our mates joined us, and at last Ratcliffe began to relax and feel a little better.

I decided it was time to find out more about him. I guessed, rightly, that like me, he was still in his teens. He came from Enfield near London and had recently learnt that his family had been killed in a Zeppelin bombing raid. He told us the story in a rather matter of fact way, which surprised us; it seemed almost as if he had nothing more to lose and didn't much care what became of him.

I asked him how he felt about the terrible treatment he was being given. He told us that he was suffering horribly and hoped that his life would end soon. Mercifully, he was given no more punishment that day; maybe even the bully knew it would have finished him off.

My mates and I felt so sorry for Ratcliffe and we were really angry with his tormentor. We talked about ways we could get the horrible man to stop his bullying, but unless we had the support of more senior officers, there was little we could do.

"Couldn't we just drop him overboard one dark night when no one is looking?" was one of the less sensible suggestions, but none of us came up with a solution. We agreed to mull over ideas, and then talk again.

The following day, the bully took Ratcliffe up on deck and ordered him to scrub the surface. The fierce conditions of the day before had subsided a little, but the weather was still appallingly bad.

"Come on, man, get down to it. What's the matter with you? Get started, now!"

Ratcliffe stood, shaking uncontrollably. I heard him say, "No, no" as he backed away, which enraged the vindictive officer further. It was clear Ratcliffe wasn't able to face this task after all the punishment he had taken at the hands of this so-called superior, and so I was left with no option but to get involved and go to his aid.

"Sir, please let him go." I spoke clearly and firmly. "I think Ratcliffe has had enough."

"Who the fuck do you think you are, White? Do you want to scrub the decks yourself?" the bully snapped back at me.

"I'm just saying Ratcliffe is exhausted and terrified. He won't be able to work outside today. Anyway, the decks don't need cleaning. The sea has done that job for us."

"You're for it now, White. You wait there, Ratcliffe, you little shit, I haven't finished with you yet. OK, we'll have it your way, White – now get down there and scrub. And you'll have to do a better job than this idiot or you really will be in trouble."

As I started to work with great difficulty, I heard a bellowed command.

"Get that man in from the decks – now!"

I wondered who was shouting, hoping it was the Captain. At least someone was there to witness my appalling treatment. I struggled to stand up and stagger back inside, slipping and skidding sideways as the ship lurched to port. I thought I was going to be washed overboard and clung on to the railings as I struggled to my feet, staggering towards the door only to be swept back once more. I waited for a lull in the rocking of the ship and finally made it inside where the bully was waiting for me, sneering and relishing my extreme discomfort, but I still didn't know who had called for me to come inside.

I was so upset and angry with the bully that I lost my composure, reaching the stage where I couldn't care less what happened to me. I raised my arm and smacked the arrogant bastard in the face as hard as I could, calling him every name under the sun. He fell back, hitting his head on the metal wall.

He sat up, stunned, shook his head, and then yelled at me, "Right, this time I'm going to get you, you fucking little sod!"

He struggled to get back on his feet. His hand touched a metal object and his face showed satisfaction as he looked down and saw it was a discarded spanner. As he palmed it, I knew exactly what his intention was; I was going to be seriously injured soon after he raised his arm.

It was at that exact moment that a deafening explosion rocked the ship and I was thrown to the floor. We were hit so suddenly and squarely on the port side that the steel plate was ripped apart and water must have been pouring into the engine room. The ship lurched dangerously over to port and we all knew it would sink to the bottom of the ocean in minutes. The sheer terror of those moments will stay with me and haunt me always.

Being highly trained, we all went swiftly into action. The Captain on the bridge called out to us to man the lifeboats. We ran towards the boats on the sloping deck and tried to free them, but they were all jammed, probably due to the force of the explosion. I called for a team to wrench one free and shouted at them to pull and heave, but however much I encouraged the men, the boats were stuck fast.

In a fleeting moment, I knew we would all have to endure the killing cold of the ocean and choke on the oil that was surely spreading on the surface, but duty and training forced me to put aside these thoughts. I looked over at the Weapons Officer who was trying to defuse the depth charges before we went down. He was fighting a losing battle and still had several dozen to work on.

I went across to help him just as the bow moved upwards. We only had minutes left. We worked as fast as we could, and when I called over to two men nearby to help us, I saw that one of them was Ratcliffe. We had around a dozen fuses left as we went down and I vaguely heard the Captain shouting at us to abandon ship.

The moment had come when every man had to look after himself. I was desperately trying to decide where to jump into the water so that I didn't hit the hull first when I heard a terrified scream to my right. Ratcliffe was grasping on to the railings and seemed to be frozen with fear, crying uncontrollably. I grabbed him by the arm and assured him that I would look after him to calm him. Fortunately, he didn't realise that I was as petrified as he was.

I had to make a quick decision. We only had a few seconds left to jump or be dragged down by the sinking ship. This was the moment I had been dreading and I prayed that I would be able to control my emotions and behave with courage. I'd always wondered how I would react in a moment of life or death. Now I was about to find out.

Would I be a hero or coward?

CHAPTER 12

Horror on the Atlantic

I put my arm around Ratcliffe's shoulders and led him towards the bow, which was still rising. I made sure we walked as I assumed this would reduce panic, in me as well as him, although instinct told me to run. He was still crying as I tightened my grip to give him confidence and spoke to him clearly and slowly.

All around us, men were jumping over the rails into the sea. I saw some hit the side of the ship, skidding down towards the keel, the plating ripping the clothes and skin off their backs and legs. Their screams were terrible.

I grabbed Ratcliffe's arm and waited for an opportunity to jump directly into the water, avoiding the fate of those other unfortunate men. And then, over the side we went. Everything happened in slow motion; it seemed an age since we'd stopped working on the fuses, but it was probably only a few seconds. We jumped together, Ratcliffe and I. I wouldn't let go of his arm as we hung in the air for a short moment, and then crashed into the sea.

Nothing prepares you for the shock of the deadly icy-cold water of the Atlantic. We both went under and struggled to get back up to the surface. As our heads broke through, we gasped and rasped for breath, and then Ratcliffe screamed. We had been warned during training that extreme cold numbs your guts, limbs and brain, making it almost impossible to think clearly and stop panicking. We didn't have long before we would freeze to death, and that would be a horrible way to go.

I kicked off my sea boots and shouted at him to do the same as I made a grab for his feet. After a struggle, I managed to free one boot, but his head went under the water, rising again as he gasped for air, choking and coughing. The swell of the waves was high and I shouted that he had to keep his head clear.

I grabbed his collar and pulled him upwards when he went under again. We were both struggling and spluttering, trying to keep breathing and stay alive. To have a chance of survival, we had to get out of the water. I managed to get Ratcliffe's other boot off. The cold started to numb every part of my body and my brain wasn't working. We desperately needed to find some floating object to climb on to. I shouted at him to keep swimming and stay above the surface.

Just then, I heard a rushing and swirling sound, and looked back to see the last of the stern as it slithered under the waves. We were swept backwards towards the rapidly disappearing ship, and for a terrifying moment, I thought we would be sucked under as we were pulled towards the metal shell and deadly propellers. Thousands of sailors had been cut to pieces on these monstrous blades. We were desperately struggling forward to get away from the whirlpool which was trying to pull us down using kicks and arm movements. Several men behind might have gone under, but I cannot be certain. Yet again, it was every man for himself.

Somehow, Ratcliffe and I managed to struggle away, and for a moment, I forgot about the cold and our dreadful situation. We had been spared for the time being.

I struck forward, still holding Ratcliffe by his shirt to keep him afloat. Several hundred yards away, some men had found a raft, and others were trying to mount planks of wood. We would have to find our own flotsam and get out of the water as soon as possible.

As the huge waves swelled up to an almost impossible height, I saw two ships coming towards us, but they were still many miles away. There was no way they would arrive in time to save us if we stayed in the water. The swell waned and we were dragged down, and then the ships were out of sight.

As we surfaced, I saw something solid sweeping past me and made a grab for it. I never imagined that I would be so grateful to hold a plank of wood in my hand. I yelled at Ratcliffe to grasp hold of the other end and get on top of it. He desperately tried to do so, but just as he pulled his chest out of the deadly water, he slipped off and the plank tipped over.

He was spluttering and crying and thrusting about in panic. I knew he didn't have much time left, so I talked to him to calm him. Eventually, I managed to get him balanced on the length of the plank with only a leg and arm still trailing in the water, and I held on to the end near his head. I was able to pull myself up, but there was no way the plank could support both of us. At least this gave me time to get my breath back and be out of immediate danger, but it would only buy me a few more moments before the water overcame me.

I had to find another way to get out of the deadly cold of the water. Making sure Ratcliffe was calm and steady, I reached out with one arm to paddle forwards, trying to drag the plank along with him on top. Fortunately, he had calmed down a bit, and so I was able to focus on my task. I was trying to reach the raft still many yards away, but I was making no progress at all.

I shouted at Ratcliffe to start paddling to help get us there, but he was frozen stiff and still plainly terrified, so I was forced to leave him and strike out for the raft on my own with an incomplete plan in my mind. Maybe I could grab a rope and go back to fetch him.

After a long, desperate struggle, I managed to reach the raft, but there wasn't room for me on top and I had to cling on to the edge, gasping for breath. I was alongside a dozen other men holding on to the edge, while eight luckier souls had managed to get out of the water. I shouted to ask if anyone had managed to find any rope, but no one replied. Everyone, understandably, was focusing solely on their own survival.

I looked back towards the whirlpool which the sunken ship had left and saw that there were dozens of men struggling to stay alive. The inevitable oil was spreading over the water and I prayed that it would not catch alight. We were perhaps a couple of hundred yards away, but I knew how dangerous the situation would be.

I had a flashback to my very first voyage when I had watched from the safety of the ship I was on as hundreds of men were swamped by burning oil, devastated that we had to leave them to their fate. Our Captain had decided that it was too dangerous to hang around to rescue them; there were still too many U-boats in the area and our ship would be a sitting duck. We ploughed through the mass of screaming men, killing many poor souls, but perhaps saving them from an even worse fate. The

Captain later collapsed under the terrible weight of responsibility and guilt and became a shaking, incoherent wreck. He was forced to retire immediately and finished up in a mental hospital.

In our present predicament, the oil had managed to calm the waters, but that was the only good news. There were dozens of men desperately trying to swim away from the spreading black mass, but most were being overtaken by it. Coughing and spluttering, they were temporarily blinded. Oil slows a person's movement in water while causing a terrible burning in their eyes and lungs, and a constant fierce retching almost rips out their stomach. Once smothered in oil, they will be kept alive for a longer time than they would in freezing water, but this only prolongs their shocking agony.

And then the fire started. The flames burnt away all the oxygen and the men in the oil struggled to breathe. We could only watch and listen to the terror and screaming as the fire approached the first swimmers, then took the middle ones. The younger men, swimming away at a faster pace, were the last to die. One man was still giving a thumbs up to his mates as he screamed in excruciating pain, burnt to a black cinder.

Having seen shipwrecked men in the water before, I prayed that none would be left alive as their burns and the effects of the oil would cause them terrible agony. I had seen plenty of men beg the medics to end their lives rather than leaving them to suffer. Others would try to cough up the oil in their lungs and suffocate.

The oil spread a little nearer to us. I felt desperate fear and hoped that I would not suffer such a terrible fate; I couldn't help thinking about my own survival and made a huge effort to remember my faith and humanity.

I looked around for Ratcliffe who I had left on the plank a couple of hundred yards back. As much as I didn't want to, I knew I would have to return to bring him closer to the raft, even though I had no rope. In my deep despair, I had no idea how I was going to do this.

Then I saw a man – I couldn't identify him to begin with – swimming towards the plank and trying to drag the rating off it. The monster! He wanted the floating plank to save his own life. Ratcliffe was trying to push him away, but the man was not giving up as he tugged and pulled at his clothing. I couldn't believe that anyone could be so cruel and selfish. He was only interested in saving himself and couldn't give a damn about anyone else.

Then the man's face turned towards me and I recognised him immediately. It was that despicable bullying Lieutenant who had made Ratcliffe's life such a misery. My blood boiled in anger and frustration, and I shouted out all the worst swear words I could think of to commend him to the devil. Eventually the bully managed to overturn the plank and poor Ratcliffe disappeared under the water.

Furious, I swam towards the plank in the hope that I could find the poor man. As I swam forward, the waves seemed to work against me, and after several minutes, I was still only a couple of yards away from the raft. I tried to swim faster, but I made even less progress. I knew I would have to give up as my efforts were hopeless, but the injustice of the scene overwhelmed me and my anger drove me to try once again. Eventually, though, I had to accept the inevitable.

As I trod water, I wasn't sorry to see the burning oil smother the devil who was now on the plank. I will never forget his screams which even drowned out the roar of the flames.

I never saw Ratcliffe again.

In deep sorrow and fierce anger, numb with cold, I slowly made my way back to the raft. The Captain, now safely on board, extended his hand when he saw me swimming back and pulled me on to the already overfull raft. I tried not to cry, but I failed. My tears flowed for the poor young rating, Ratcliffe, whose life had ended before it had even begun. And I cried for myself, too. I was so relieved to be out of the water at last, but had no reserves of energy left at all.

I sat up on the raft gratefully, and then looked back towards where the ship had been. Horrified, I saw the oil spreading towards us and knew the flames would not be far behind.

CHAPTER 13

Enigma

I woke up and groaned as I became aware of my soaking bedding. Exhausted after my recurring nightmare, I sat up in bed, afraid to fall asleep again and recall those terrible memories.

I hated being shut away in my cabin; I had a terrible fear that the next torpedo would blast through the thin steel plating by my bunk and I would have to relive the horrors of being shipwrecked all over again. The water would rush in and I would have little chance to get up on deck to safety. I would be drowned in seconds like a trapped rat. No, I didn't want to stay down here, but I didn't want to go up to the bridge either.

I looked at my tired face in the mirror, at the baggy black smudges under my eyes. I was exhausted, but there would be no let up until this mission was over. I doubted if there were any seamen who were not suffering in some way. They were certainly all dog tired.

I sat down in my deep armchair to think about my poor men and the constant demands being made on them. After the horrible experiences that had given birth to my nightmares, I hated being at sea and had never wanted to get back on to a ship again. I had lost my nerve and hoped I wouldn't become institutionalised like the poor Captain who'd had to order his crew to leave shipwrecked men stranded to die a horrible death. My hands were trembling; it was impossible to control them.

Oh God, what will become of me?

My naval career began in the midst of World War I, and since then I have sailed on all seven oceans. As I became more competent, I climbed the promotional ladder and had been very excited about my future. Where had it all gone wrong? I couldn't impose my wrecked body and mind on to an innocent young woman, although I missed Isla terribly. No woman should have to be burdened by a decrepit old man with a disintegrating mind. Perhaps after all this was over, I could settle into a home for retired seamen.

With a massive effort, I got dressed and made my way to the stairs. I climbed slowly up to the bridge where the Captain was standing. The sea was a bit calmer than it had been and we were able to talk without being thrown around the small space.

We were both offered mugs of cocoa which we gratefully accepted.

"When do you think we should break away from the convoy?" the Captain asked. I wasn't sure yet. We were here for a special mission – my mission – but we were also part of the protection group for the convoy.

"It depends. If we don't suffer any more attacks in the next couple of days, I think that will be the time to travel north," I replied, but I was unsatisfied with my answer. I would only know the right time when my gut feeling told me.

I stayed on the bridge with the Captain, looking at weather reports. The seas would become rougher by morning, but the radar was showing no evidence of uninvited guests and the ASDIC was quiet.

"If things stay as they are, we could slip away tomorrow. Might be our best chance." I had talked through the options with the Captain and he knew our mission almost as well as I did. We were to find the German weather ship, *Wuppertal*, and capture and board her before the crew had time to destroy their code books, if indeed they had any. But I was certain they did. If our mission was successful, it would be the first time we had been able to obtain the Enigma secrets from the enemy.

I sent a radio message to base to get an updated position for *Wuppertal*. While I was waiting for a reply, the Captain was called away to the engine room, and now I had a little time to reflect on all that had happened over the past few months.

My thoughts when I'd stepped on to the train at London Euston, having found myself a quiet carriage, had centred on Isla and how I would miss her enormously. She was quite the loveliest lady I had met in a long time, perhaps ever. No, *definitely* ever! I loved her elegant good looks and the strong structure of her cheekbones and determined jutting chin, giving her a classical style. She carried herself with the poise of a film star, but in a more subtle way, and when she arranged her luscious auburn hair so that it was swept up sideways and clasped under her cap, she became a goddess in my eyes. But she was understated and not flashy in any way. Her glamour was subtle and I loved her gentle style.

Isla's keen intelligence was also evident and she led her group sessions and meetings with skill and charm. Above all, I loved her character with her dry humour and clever asides. And as for those brown eyes, they were so deep and passionate. She looked truly fabulous in her Wren's uniform.

We hadn't started a relationship yet as we hadn't had the time or opportunity, hardly ever meeting without others around us, but I was determined that I would make the time, pluck up the courage and arrange to meet her away from work when I got back to England. I was sure we both shared the same feelings; we'd had one significant meeting in the canteen just before I left when we said so much without words, which I valued immensely. When at last we could get together, we would have plenty to talk about. We hadn't even had the chance to share information about our families, our hopes and ambitions. I just couldn't wait to get to know her better, but fervently hoped that she wouldn't see into my soul and find an empty space. I hoped she wouldn't get to discover my broken mind and body.

Perhaps we could ride to a local pub on my motorbike, but I would have to ensure I cleaned every part of it carefully first. The thought that I might stain this beautiful lady's clothes was abhorrent to me.

Our age difference worried me; I must be twice her age. Maybe when she considered this, she would have her doubts as well. Surely Isla would get tired of an old man. If we had children, I wouldn't get to kick a football around with them until I was in my fifties and I'd be greeting my grandchildren into the world in my seventies. This played on my mind and caused me great concern.

I cursed my weakness in not speaking to Isla directly about my feelings for her; I hadn't even had the courage to ask her to walk with me in the grounds. We stayed in separate accommodation, of course, and worked long hours, so we had little opportunity to meet up socially. However, I was determined to find a way and I wouldn't waste any more time. I had a long train journey to think about us and plan for my return.

The train was pulling into Liverpool Lime Street Station when it occurred to me that I hadn't made time to think about my new adventure at all. While part of me dreaded going to sea again – my body and mind had suffered enough – I had to focus on the mission. I cursed myself for not using the valuable time the train journey had afforded me for planning ahead, although my team and I had already spent hours going through every detail. I had also gone over the procedures with my bosses at the Admiralty and knew them by heart, but this mission was so important not just to me and my team, but to thousands of men and tons of valuable goods.

I knew my way to Gladstone Dock having travelled there many times before and took a bus for the short journey. I spotted my ship even before I had seen her name: she was the brightest frigate there and had just received one of the most comprehensive refurbishments ever by order of the Admiralty, as requested by me. I wanted the most up-to-date equipment and weaponry, including the latest radar, ASDIC and depth charge projector, and I was insistent that the refurbishment covered every area inside and out. Now this grand lady, HMS *Derwent*, was sparkling.

After climbing aboard, I reported to Captain Oliver who saluted me. He then showed me proudly around his ship, pointing out all the additions and improvements. I was impressed and knew that we were well prepared for the mission.

I had arranged special training for the ship and her company, planning for us to travel to Scapa Flow for a couple of days away together with the corvette HMS *Orchid*. The following day, our two ships made their way north and I watched out for the familiar sights, looking across to the northern part of the Wirral. As we sailed, I had a good view of the famous Blackpool Tower and the town's sandy beaches, and then the huge granite Chicken Rock Lighthouse just off the Isle of Man.

By the time we moved out into the open sea, I had almost forgotten the terrors and thrills of the Atlantic Ocean as our ship lurched through the swells and troughs. After almost fifteen months ashore, I had also forgotten the shock of the fierce cold and the biting winds, the tension we all felt, the anticipation of a U-boat attack.

A retired Admiral had set up a small training facility in a bay near Scapa Flow to prepare the teams for our mission. I was extremely impressed with his toughness and thoroughness and knew we would have the best preparation under his direction. I'd wanted to spend a month training here, but I was under great pressure from the Admiralty for early results. After just one week, our two ships were due to cross the Atlantic to meet up with the convoy leaving Newfoundland and provide protection. At least, that's what we wanted the enemy to believe.

Two weeks later, we had already lost two ships from the convoy. The first, a corvette, was just a few hundred yards behind us. Fortunately, as the escort ship sank, most of the men had enough time to make it to the lifeboats. Others had jumped into the sea; some unlucky ones were overcome by the oil which spread on the surface, but others were rescued by the *Derwent* and nearby ships.

The second ship we lost was a vast tanker and its crew were not so lucky. The torpedo had instantly ignited the oil she was carrying, and the resulting blast lit up the sky and ocean as if we were in the middle of a sunny day. Flames shot for miles up into the heavens.

"Poor bastards, they never had a chance," the man standing to my right said, rather unnecessarily. This was Captain Oliver's first command, but certainly not his first experience of the devastation the U-boats caused on an almost daily basis. He was younger than me, but I had respect for the way he managed his men and ship. I liked him, although I would have preferred a man with more experience.

Including escorts, we now had twenty-three ships in the convoy. Apart from losing our precious men in the explosion, we'd also lost vast quantities of oil, weapons and food destined for British shores. I felt guilty that we would have to leave the convoy, together with our corvette, in a couple of days, meaning even less protection for our ships.

The crew hadn't managed to avenge the losses and fight back against the U-boats, but were determined to do so when the opportunity arose. The ASDIC had picked up the pings of at least four U-boats, but despite launching dozens of depth charges overboard, we hadn't made any hits. Now the U-boats had got away without a dent and would probably come back tonight, seeking more spoils.

The following morning, our two ships, *Derwent* and *Orchid*, turned away to the north and left the convoy behind. I hoped that the U-boats would not notice our departure and we could get to the *Wuppertal* unobserved.

I signalled the Admiralty, asking for an updated position of the *Wuppertal*, and reported this to the Captain when it arrived. I also kept in contact with Bletchley on a daily basis, wondering if it was Isla who received my messages, and relayed all the information I received to *Orchid* two miles behind us.

We were three days away from our target. The *Derwent* took a wide passage around the position of the *Wuppertal,* and when we had completed a semi-circle, we switched off our engines – I had ordered radio silence – and waited out of sight until the *Orchid* was on the far side. We could now approach the weather ship from opposite sides. Both ships planned to get to the *Wuppertal* just before light the following morning, exploiting the element of surprise before the crew panicked.

At the appointed time, the *Orchid* and *Derwent* each launched a whaler. I was leading the whaler from the *Derwent* with seven crew members as we rowed silently towards the *Wuppertal*. It was a cold, misty morning, but dawn was only minutes away. To my relief, the sea was calm. The crew was silent; no one was even allowed to sneeze.

I felt more nervous than I had been for many years. The next few moments would spell the success or failure of the mission. Speed, stealth and surprise would give us the best chance. I prayed that we would be successful as so much depended on this.

I watched the ship through my binoculars as the sky became a little brighter, praying that we would not be noticed before we reached her. My heart was beating much faster than usual and I looked down at my hands, which were shaking again. After months of preparation, we were only two hundred yards away.

It was then that I heard a shout from the ship and saw a man waving on the deck. In moments, two other men had joined him. I watched carefully to see what they would do, speaking urgently in a low voice, telling my men to row faster. But I knew instinctively that the day was lost, and my fears were realised when I saw a man I presumed to be the Captain throw a weighted bag overboard.

"Oh, bugger it!" I shouted out loud. Then I saw the Captain staggering over to the side with what looked like a large typewriter, which he dropped into the water as well. This was my first sighting of an Enigma machine; I had no doubt it was the machine I was desperate to capture.

At least now we knew that the weather ships carried the machines as well. This would be useful intelligence for Bletchley, but it alone was not worth the huge expense and massive effort of planning and setting up this mission. I was bitterly disappointed.

In moments, we'd approached the side of the ship. I reached up for a hand hold and climbed aboard, followed by four of my armed seamen. The men from the other whaler would be boarding on the far side at exactly the same moment, as we had practised so many times at Scapa Flow. The Captain of the ship greeted us as we climbed aboard, which I thought was rather strange. I pointed my gun at his chest and ordered him to move aside as my men rushed on to the bridge where I suspected the paperwork was kept.

I left the Captain looking rather bemused. A quick search confirmed that the bridge was clear, so I led my men on to the Captain's quarters.

A couple of men from the other whaler went below decks to look for and disconnect any scuttling charges the German crew might have laid, while the rest rounded up the crew members on deck. Most of the German sailors had rushed to jump overboard in panic. We had no need to shoot any of them; they were terrified of us.

While the approach and boarding of the *Wuppertal* had gone to plan, I had missed the opportunity to capture our first Enigma machine. It and the code books in their weighted bags had gone overboard. In frustration, I pulled out the drawers of the Captain's desk and emptied their contents on to the floor. My team frantically tore papers out of the files; some bunches were tied with string, which they ripped apart.

Within minutes, we'd found what we were looking for – Enigma code books for previous months. The Captain must only have had time to dispose of the current month's books. Bletchley had never seen copies of these, and I don't mind admitting that I whooped with joy! The mission had been a success after all.

CHAPTER 14

Love Blooms at Bletchley Park

I was at the back of the room when my beautiful man walked in. There must have been one hundred of us there ready to give him a big welcome, and we all stood up together and clapped and cheered at the tops of our voices. This was our greatest moment and biggest breakthrough after so many months of struggle and failure.

We all congratulated this clever and resourceful man, but my cheers were for a totally different reason. Tam had come back safely and life was worth living again. The sun had returned to my world. I had never felt more exhilarated. Of course, I was incredibly proud of him and his achievements, but I hadn't been able to sleep while he was away, unable to make contact with me.

I hadn't taken any of my colleagues into my confidence about my feelings for Tam. I suppose I was used to keeping my innermost thoughts to myself, having spent most of my childhood alone, and he was such a hero to us all, some of the other girls may have felt the same way about him and I didn't want to cause any friction in the team. However, two of my good friends had noticed how down I had become and asked me what was wrong. They guessed a man was involved, but didn't know who he was. I denied that anything was wrong, but in truth, I had felt wretched inside.

Now Tam was back, we couldn't waste any more time. The next day, I managed to sit on the same table as him in the canteen. As some of the other women were with us, I spoke to him about the codes and asked him what the next steps would be. When the other girls realised that they were not included in the conversation, they drifted away, and I had my gorgeous man to myself.

We looked at each other in disbelief and I waited for him to pluck up the courage to open the conversation. For a brave and resourceful man, he was painfully shy when it came to affairs of the heart. In the end, I decided I had to speak.

"I am so happy you are safely back with me. I missed you dreadfully and desperately hope you feel the same way about me. If you do, I don't think we should waste any more time."

I hadn't read the signs wrongly before he left for his mission; Tam did have feelings for me. Oh, the joy! It was indescribable.

The following week, we both had the afternoon off. At his suggestion, I got on the back of his bike, clean and shiny for the occasion, which was not easy in my tight Wren's uniform. The day was blowy with intermittent sun, but it was perfect for us. I had to pinch myself to believe that we were finally out together on our own.

We rode into the countryside for a picnic I had prepared, looking forward to lovely private time to get to know each other. I had packed a few sandwiches and a bottle of orange squash, and he'd put the bag into a side pocket on the bike with badly frayed straps. His bike was quite powerful and made a throaty rasping noise with occasional shotgun blasts. I had never been on a motorbike before and was not sure what to expect.

We went at an alarming pace and my bottom was forced backwards on the seat. I wrapped my arms around Tam and held on tightly as I was in danger of falling off, screaming in shock as he accelerated even more; I was certain that we were going to crash. The wind blew in our faces and I heard a ripping sound. Looking down, I was terrified that some vital part of my clothing had burst open. Fortunately, it was not me, but the pocket holding our picnic. The high speed had torn the straps and our cucumber sandwiches and bottle had disappeared on to the road behind us. I shouted out to Tam that we had lost our lunch and we roared with laughter, both exhilarated by the loveliness of the moment.

I enjoyed one of the most beautiful days of my life as we talked and talked about our families, hopes and dreams. Tam came from a place called Tain on the north-eastern coast of Scotland, not far from Inverness. He told me about the long horizons and beautiful light, the land of good earth and wild weather. His home was shown off at its best when the sun shone through the clean air. He described the wholesome and healthy environment and recommended the whisky as a good antidote for the cold weather! I longed to visit his hometown with him.

He had been brought up by his mother, who was still alive, and he regretted having so little time to visit her. His father had been a seaman who had left home when Tam was three. He had no siblings.

"I always had a yearning to go to sea as soon as I was old enough," he told me. "I thought if I could keep moving across the oceans, I would one day find my father. I didn't, of course."

"Where did you get the name Tam – is it a family name? I've never heard it before. It's most unusual."

"Yes, my father was called Tam; it's a Scottish version of Thomas. My mother is called Morven and she was a much-loved schoolteacher, until she had to spend her time looking after me. She is an extremely clever woman, and luckily for me, she spent valuable time on my education. She taught me mathematics in all its forms and insisted I became perfect in each subject, drumming the knowledge into me until I absorbed it freely. I had a thirst for learning. It was she who instilled in me my love for crosswords, but however good I get, I could never surpass her."

Tam asked me about my childhood and background and I gave him a short summary of my life so far. Then I asked him about his life at sea.

"When did you join the Navy?"

"I was sixteen years old. After basic training, I became a junior rating on a corvette sailing out of Glasgow on the Clyde. We were escorting troop ships to Egypt during World War I. The U-boats were still causing immense damage to our ships and took the lives of thousands of our men, and for a young seaman, it was terrifying, but I learned my trade and gained promotion as my experience broadened.

"On my third trip in the Atlantic, my ship was sunk. I survived, but only just. It was the most horrible experience, and today hundreds of our seamen are still suffering the same terrors. That's why I am determined to help eradicate the menace of the U-boats. After the Great War, I stayed on in the Navy, mostly serving in the Far East. As you know, I've served in the Atlantic since the start of this war.

"The sea is the place I wanted to be and I loved the work and the camaraderie, but I think I have had enough now. It seems like I have been involved in war for as long as I can remember. It's such a terrible waste of lives and achieves nothing in the longer term.

"I was on the first Russian convoy in 41 and I will never forget it. We shouldn't have had to endure the inhuman conditions we were subjected to. On a later convoy, the crew mutinied and most of the survivors finished up in institutions, their minds ruined for life, despite the skills of the doctors. Humans aren't designed to cope with such physical and mental hardships...

"But I won't waste our precious time together going into any more detail. I just hope that no one will ever have to go through these conditions again."

"Has there ever been anyone special in your life?" I asked him.

"I was married once, but unfortunately it was a disaster. We lived in London, which was where she was from, but I was away for long periods of time. Her mother lived with us, and she and I didn't get on at all. She dominated the house, and every time I came home on leave, she would get between us. My wife didn't seem to notice the problem, but I certainly did – it didn't feel like married life at all. Her mother was always interfering and criticising and never stopped complaining, and I became obsessed with the dreadful thought that my wife, who I loved very much at one time, would turn out like the old woman.

"Then I found out that another man had moved in while I was away. I caught him in the house with her – and her mother, of course – and thought good luck to them. All three of them. I walked away with my few possessions and never went back. I now look on this as a lucky escape!"

I laughed at the humorous way he told his story, but it was a tragic tale. At that moment, I loved him deeply, but I couldn't help worrying about Tam meeting my mother. What would his reaction be? Would he be disappointed, thinking I was going to turn out as acerbic, and leave? No, of course he wouldn't. He wasn't like that. Actually, they would probably get on well as they were both clever and educated people and both from Scotland.

I had no worries at all about Tam meeting my father. At that moment, I decided I would introduce him to them at the earliest opportunity, but that might be months away. I wouldn't tell my parents about Tam in the meantime.

"I can't really blame her, though," Tam was still talking about his wife. "It can be tough being married to a sailor, especially an old salt like me."

He grinned rather self-consciously. I was sure I would have no problems being married to him, but I kept quiet. I wondered if they had divorced, and if not, did he intend to arrange this?

He seemed to read my mind. "Fortunately, there were no children. If there had been, I would never have left. I couldn't walk away from my own children. We are not divorced yet, even though I left more than five years ago, but I will make sure it happens when the time is right." He looked at me and smiled. Was the time right now? I hoped so!

The day passed quickly as I was totally absorbed with this lovely man. I couldn't believe that it was already six o'clock and the air was cooling. We were both hungry having missed out on our lovely picnic lunch, but if he had asked me to stay there with him for the evening, or indeed for the whole night, I would not have hesitated for a moment. But our duties meant that we needed to be back at Bletchley. We would have to work until ten at least, and maybe longer if there was a flap on.

We reluctantly got back on to the lovely old bike. The return journey was as precious a memory as the rest of the afternoon had been, even though the ride still frightened me witless. I will never forget that day out, even many decades on.

Back at Bletchley, Tam was becoming obsessed with the idea of stealing an Enigma machine from a U-boat.

"This would make all the difference to the outcome of the war. We must get hold of one of those damned machines."

We spent hours planning how to achieve this, deciding on a course of action and even creating a pool with model boats to simulate the exercise. Our plan was to damage a U-boat enough to force it to surface and the crew to climb up the conning tower. They would then have the grim choice between jumping overboard or being shot by our destroyer's machine guns.

Our men would have to be careful and quick, taking great care to ensure that no weighted bags were dumped into the sea as they rushed on board and captured the prize of the Enigma and all the associated paperwork. We would have to avoid damaging the ship too much; we didn't want it to sink before we had a chance to plunder it. Ideally, we wanted to tow it back to Britain, which would need a combination of skill and luck.

During days of preparation, I knew that Tam would have to leave again soon. I couldn't believe we would be apart once more and didn't think I could bear the loneliness of being without him. We only had one more occasion to meet privately before he went, although our relationship was common knowledge by then which made things a little easier.

Tam insisted on working with *Derwent* and *Orchid* again, recruiting as many of the same crew members as last time as possible. The ships were in Scapa Flow, and once more Tam arranged for intensive training for his men so that they could perfect the operation. As before, they only had one short week to spare.

Tam was looking forward to the trip and was determined to get his machine. His life now had new purpose and he was excited about getting back safely to plan our future together. However, hopes and dreams don't always come to fruition.

CHAPTER 15

A Hero's Death

I was terrified about going to sea again and promised myself that this would be my last voyage. My mind and body couldn't take much more punishment, and I wanted to get back to Isla and start planning our lives together on land. I would need to find an occupation – if, of course, we won the war – but Isla was sure I could get a good job with my mental abilities. She convinced me that my skills would be in great demand in the new world of peace. The government and businesses would need clever people to develop the technologies of the future.

But that was all a dream for the moment.

The best way to attract the U-boats was to travel with convoys once again, so we sailed to Boston to meet up with nineteen ships loaded with food, men and ammunition. We spent hours gazing at the ASDIC machines, looking for tell-tale signs of U-boats, preferably one operating alone. Sometimes we would get positive signs and spend hours trying to locate them, firing off dozens of depth charges to find nothing.

"Bastard got away. Let's keep searching." I would encourage my men to keep going after early disappointments. All the while, packs of U-boats were still causing havoc and we lost half our ships from the convoy. Fortunately, we were able to pick up most of the men safely from the water.

After several days of patient observation, trial and error, we fired our charges following another signal and a huge explosion threw hundreds of tons of water into the air. We watched as the dreaded oil spread on the surface – we had made a direct hit. While that meant there was one less menace on the seas, we were no nearer to achieving our goal.

At last, we tracked down a lone U-boat and followed it for three days. Learning from our intensive training, we dropped single charges overboard every five minutes and waited for a reaction. After one muffled explosion, our two ships, *Derwent* and *Orchid*, paused opposite each other, perhaps a mile apart. We hoped that the U-boat would eventually surface between us.

I looked across at *Orchid* and at the sea between us. This time, she would be back-up support rather than required to launch a boat. I stared at the green and black water and the huge swells, wondering if at last this was our moment, praying the enemy vessel would soon break the surface. In anticipation, I even imagined it doing so and ordered the whaler and eight men into the water, climbing in with them.

The cold was terrible that morning and the swell was dangerously high; I hoped we wouldn't fall into the deadly water. I dreaded the waves splashing over the side of the boat, which was rocking dangerously, and wished I had put on another couple of layers. But maybe this would have made movement more difficult.

I ordered the men to row out in the direction of *Orchid,* and then, when I thought we had gone too far, we rowed back towards the ship we had left. We waited for an hour, two hours, but there was still no sign of the U-boat we hoped had been damaged by our explosives.

After a third hour had gone past, one of my men shouted and I turned to look where he was pointing. I was hardly able to believe my eyes. A huge conning tower was slowly rising out of the water, growing bigger by the minute. I was the last man to see it and cursed my lack of concentration.

Urging my rowers towards the emerging vessel, I shouted at the Lewis machine gunners on the *Derwent* to open fire. I heard the ping of the bullets bouncing off the metal of the conning tower and saw sparks flying where they made contact, the sound of the ricochet fleetingly reminding me of the Westerns which attracted huge audiences in cinemas. The conning tower was now fully free and I watched as the vast deck emerged and the seawater drained away. The noise inside the tower must have been deafening and would hopefully cause the men inside to panic.

Sure enough, a head appeared out of the opening, followed by others. They scrambled down and most jumped into the sea. When the Captain emerged, I ordered my men to continue shooting and watched as his chest exploded and blood sprayed out. The bullets blasted the leg off another man and he screamed to be spared. I could hear the German word for surrender – *kamerad* – shouted at us, but I told my men to keep firing.

I was watching carefully to see if any of the emerging men were carrying bags, pleased to see that so far, there were none. My treasure was still in the vessel. The men were jumping overboard, and those still on the deck had their arms pointing skyward. I had no qualms about shooting these men who had been utterly ruthless and without compassion. There were so many occasions in the past when they'd sunk our ships, but the cruel bastards would never stop for survivors – one Captain was asked why he hadn't picked anyone up and he claimed not to have seen them. So, we blasted away enthusiastically with no guilty feelings.

So far, our mission appeared to be going well. As I urged my rowers towards the stricken vessel, the swells were getting larger and I could see that we were going to have difficulty securing the whaler to the U-boat. The whaler crashed into it with a splintering noise and I was afraid that the damage would cause us to sink.

We failed on the first two attempts to secure the whaler to the vessel, but on the third try, we were successful. We roped up to the railings as our boat crashed repeatedly against the metal hull and tried to tie it tighter to reduce the impact of each wave.

I signalled to my ship to send a second whaler in case ours sank, then scrambled on board the deck of the U-boat, followed by two of my men, a tool kit and several empty bags. In my rush to reach the conning tower, I slipped in the blood of the enemy and crashed to the deck. Cursing with the pain, I struggled to my feet and limped the rest of the way with a badly twisted ankle.

Ignoring the pain, I pulled myself up the ladder, followed by my men. I was the first down the tower, and as I climbed through the narrow channel, I fleetingly wondered if there were any crew members left down below. I was exposed and would have had no defence if someone had stabbed upwards, but I was too full of adrenalin and excitement to care. My long-awaited prize was only a few feet away.

I reached the long room and found it deserted. The Enigma machine was sitting on the large table, looking just like a giant typewriter screwed tightly to the wooden base. I emptied my tool bag and picked out two screwdrivers.

The man following me jumped down seconds later and we worked furiously to free the machine, but it was fixed tightly to the wood. Meanwhile, a third man came down the ladder: his job was to check the boat for any stragglers and find out if the crew had set scuttling charges. If they had, he would dismantle them, and then leave.

Once again, I cursed as I put all of my strength into releasing the first screw. As it began to loosen, the U-boat lurched to starboard, throwing us across the table. We heard the metal plates of the vessel grinding as they twisted under huge pressure – the U-boat was sinking.

Sure enough, the fore of the ship began to slip downward and we held on to the table to stay upright. The ship's plates crackled and snapped, making terrifying groaning sounds like some prehistoric monster. We only had minutes to collect our treasure and get out.

At last, we removed all the screws and lifted the machine, passing it up to the third crew member who was now waiting halfway up the conning tower.

"Jim, take hold of this," I shouted. "Pass it on to the lad on the deck as quickly as possible and tell him to get it on to the boat intact. And hurry! This is more valuable than gold."

I then addressed the man working with me. "Tony, grab all the paperwork you can find and help me stuff these bags. Come on, hurry, for God's sake."

We grabbed a bag each and scooped the paperwork off the flat table. When each bag was full, we passed them on to Jim in the tower. There was a huge volume of files and paperwork, but every piece might hold important information that could save lives and bring the war to an end. We worked feverishly, and Jim had to carry two bags at a time up to the rating outside.

Water was pouring in through the damaged plates, but we could only hear it; we couldn't see the damage, which was further down the dark corridor. A hole must have been blown by our depth charge, forcing the U-boat crew to surface. I had wanted to capture and tow the boat back to land, but that would not now be possible.

The lights flickered and cut out. Yet again, I cursed. We couldn't possibly complete our task in darkness. Then, by some miracle, the lights came back on again, albeit dimly, and we resumed our frantic work.

The grinding, screaming and cracking of the dying ship deafened me and muddled my senses, and I had to force myself to concentrate. We wouldn't get out of here alive if we didn't leave immediately, but I didn't even consider doing this. The job had to be finished.

"Sir, we need to get out now. Come on!" Tony screamed desperately.

"No, we must finish the job." I was shouting to get Tony to concentrate and carry on with our vital work, but he took no notice of me and rushed towards the tower. I struggled after him, almost collapsing due to the pain in my leg, and managed to grab him by the collar, pulling him roughly back to the table.

"Get on with the fucking job, Tony. Show some bloody guts! Quick, get another bag – here!"

As I thrust a bag into the reluctant man's hands, Tony was crying.

"We are going to die, Tam, if we don't get out now."

"And thousands more will die if we leave. Stop arguing and get on with it, you stupid bastard."

And we carried on with our important work, packing bags and throwing them up the conning tower to Jim's waiting hands. Each time he climbed to the top, he threw the bags to the lad on the deck, who in turn threw them into the whaler. Although damaged through constant banging against the hull, this boat apparently wasn't in immediate danger of sinking, unlike the vessel we were inside. Jim called out to tell us that the second boat was now on its way to act as a backup. I was relieved to hear his good news.

The lights flickered again, but stayed on dimly. Sweat was pouring off my head and body, but I hardly noticed. I saw that Tony was in the last stages of exhaustion. We were still working frantically and only had about two more bags' worth of paper and files to pack and our mission would be complete. Then we could escape from our metal prison.

There was a terrible cracking and snapping sound as the metal sheets tore apart and more water rushed in. I knew then that we couldn't get the last two bags out, and I had left it too late to save myself and my two brave men, Tony and Jim.

We only had seconds to live.

In my last moments, I thought about Isla and the life we could have had. Perhaps after all, I had been too old for her and she would have tired of me. Then I blocked this negative thought from my head, wanting to be positive in my final precious moment on Earth. We would have been happy, always.

I saw images of our children, glowing like a pair of angels, a boy and a girl. She was no more than five or six and he was only a couple of years older. Isla was standing behind them, holding them fondly. The image was so clear that I reached out to touch them...

A huge torrent of water crashed through the ship and the men trapped inside were crushed, pulverised as the stern of the boat lifted and slid quickly and smoothly to the bottom of the ocean. There, three heroes would lie buried in their metal tomb for eternity.

CHAPTER 16

New Hope

I fainted when I heard the news. The blood rushed out of my head and I was sick like a child. Hands grabbed me and took me to a rest room nearby and laid me on a mattress on the floor.

I came round minutes later, feeling really dreadful. Someone helped me to drink a glass of water and I spluttered out the first few gulps.

"Isla, I'll take you back to our quarters," I heard a voice say from far away.

Within minutes, we were on the bus for the twenty-minute journey to our dormitory, where I lay awake and cried softly. I had often imagined this situation in the past. After all, these were dangerous times and men on active service, whether on land, sea or in the air, risked their lives all the time. But the reality was even more dreadful than my mind could possibly have comprehended. It was impossible to believe that I had lost my wonderful man and all our hopes and dreams would never now happen. There would be no country cottage. There would be no children; we'd even had names for them. We would never become parents or grandparents.

Poor, poor Tam, my sweet man. Did you suffer? Were you in pain? Surely you never felt any pain. It was too quick, wasn't it? I couldn't bear it if you had suffered; I would have much preferred to take your pain. I'm so sorry, Tam. You deserved a happy life with me and our family. You were a good man and the best things should have happened to you; you – we – don't deserve this ending. Nothing matters anymore. I don't care about the war and I couldn't care less what becomes of me and our country because nothing other than you counts for anything.

Oh, Tam! I heard you were so brave. You risked your own safety getting on to that sinking boat, and then you gave your life just so that we would have the knowledge to defeat the vicious enemies. You gave us our Enigma machine and almost a hundredweight of paper and files, but you always did have fierce determination to succeed and you never gave up. This was a most unselfish act and typical of your good nature. I hope all your colleagues and friends appreciate your ultimate sacrifice.

But why did it have to be you? You, dear man, deserve the biggest medal we can get for you and the personal congratulations of Churchill and the King.

But I knew this could never happen.

Everything Tam had done would have to be kept quiet so that the enemy, even many years after the war, would never know. Even in my distressed state, I could see the logic when it was explained to me patiently and caringly by a senior naval officer. None of the men killed would be recognised in any way, neither would the young man on the deck who had thrown dozens of bags into the rowing boat and, despite the huge swells, never missed. As the U-boat sank, he jumped into the sea and was picked up later. I would never get to meet him, but recognised that his actions were equally heroic.

After a few days of rest, I had to get up, put on a brave face and go back to work. My colleagues deserved my support as pressures increased. We had a mountain of paperwork to read and analyse, and as the results slowly came through, we were even more amazed at how much information Tam and his men had obtained. We now knew the position of the German *Milch* ships which refuelled the U-boats, and these were quickly identified and destroyed by our Navy. U-boats now had to make much longer journeys to refuel, which took them out of the killing area. We knew their routes and pack information, their battle plans and strategies, and slowly we began to gain the upper hand.

As a result of the sacrifice made by Tam and his men, many more of our ships came across the Atlantic unscathed and we were able to transport soldiers safely into the European battlefields. It made me so proud that Tam had made all this possible, but the irony was that no one outside our circle, apart from senior men in high office, had a clue what he had achieved and how it had been done. But there was a bright side to the secrecy – the enemy had no idea that we had seized all this information, either.

I remember travelling to Germany after the war to dismantle some of the country's more recent coding machines. A senior German Intelligence Officer told me how proud he was of the work they'd done and boasted that we'd never found out any information about their systems or machinery. He maintained that although the Germans had lost the war, they had won the intelligence. I wasn't allowed to tell him that we'd known all their secrets and codes, but I was dying to, just to wipe the smirk off his face, the arrogant b.....d. (Well, I couldn't use bad language, could I? Never out of the mouths of sweet Wrens!)

In my private moments, I grieved for Tam and swore that I would never forget him. I was allowed to keep his private papers and wrote to his mother in Scotland. She had, of course, been officially informed about his death, but I told her I very much wanted to meet her and let her know how much I'd loved and cherished Tam.

I worked every day and volunteered for extra duties to keep my mind occupied; I didn't want to spend time on my own with nothing to do but live with the pain of my loss. But each night, I cried myself to sleep. I knew I looked awful, pale and sunken-eyed, and I was sure I had lost weight. My friends were shocked at my appearance and tried to help as much as they could, but I gained little comfort from them. I visited the medics at Bletchley, but they just gave me tablets to aid my sleep. It seemed nothing could help me.

Apart from one thing. Just before Tam left, he had given me a signet ring which had belonged to his grandmother. It was exquisite, so beautifully crafted and perfectly formed in its simplicity. It reminded me so much of Tam and brought happy memories rushing back whenever I looked at it.

But life went on, despite my intense grief.

My great friend Eva, who I'd first met at the domestic science college in Devon, had written to me, inviting me to stay with her family in Felixstowe. We frequently exchanged letters and I had told her about my loss without giving away any details. We hadn't met up for over a year, but I had some leave due and my boss was nagging me to take time off and enjoy a change of scenery.

Eva and I agreed to meet up at her mother's house the following week. It took an age to get there by train, but it was worth it to see the beautiful countryside and the blue sea. I was made to feel so welcome during my stay in her home. Despite rationing, her mother Amelia managed to feed us with local food, and this was a huge treat for me after the terrible diet at Bletchley. We even had fresh fish direct from the harbour, which was a super treat.

As we went for long walks in the beautiful Suffolk countryside and along the flat seashore, Eva told me that she was now working as a cookery teacher for young mothers, applying much of her learning from the college in Devon. This time, it was the students she was calling cretins! Her sister Rosa was a Land Girl, and I spent many happy hours working with her in the fields. It was harvest time and we had to cut the wheat and separate the corn. Every morning, we joined other girls to milk the cows and sell the milk locally. Not having refrigeration, we had to turn the remainder of the milk into butter and cheese.

We didn't have much modern farming equipment and most of the work was done by hand, but we did have a brand-new tractor which had been imported from America. I loved to drive this beautiful machine, which was great for pulling the trailer of heavy bales into the barn.

It was essential to keep the rabbit population down due to the damage they were doing to the crops and we enjoyed delicious rabbit stews in the evening as a result. During the hot afternoons, we'd stop for a very welcome cider break. This delicious drink, which I had never tried before, was made from apples grown on the farm.

I had never been involved in agricultural work before and it was an education for me. The work was exhausting and tough, and I was so tired by early evening that I'd go to bed and fall into a deep sleep until I had to get up again at five. But I loved the country life, and after a hard few days, I felt invigorated. I hardly even had time to think about Tam; I didn't mention him to the other girls as many had suffered losses of their own in the war, and I didn't want to add to their grief. The plentiful sun, fresh air and summer breeze coloured my cheeks and arms, and my depression lifted at least temporarily.

Eva was still an outgoing character and knew several of the airmen in the local US Airforce camp. She would invite them to the house and her mother never complained about the noise or the extra food she had to find. Every visit would turn into a party, and the men brought plenty of beer and presents of stockings with them for us girls. One even brought a gramophone and we played modern tunes on 78 records.

Eva always made sure to invite one particular man, even though he was quieter than the others. From

Texas, Gerry talked about becoming a lawyer when he returned home. I could tell that Eva and he were becoming close; even though she denied it, I sometimes felt I was a little bit in the way when they were together.

Sometime later, Gerry brought Eva to London, and they invited her younger brother Philip and me to join them. We thoroughly enjoyed several evenings out in the West End, dancing in many places. Mostly, though, we just enjoyed drinks and chatter and laughter – the American Bar at the Savoy was a favourite haunt. We were happy to be alive and didn't allow the frequent sirens and bombing raids to spoil our fun.

I particularly remember going to the Queensberry Club one night when Glenn Miller was playing. Eva was mad keen on his music and managed to get his autograph. The following week, Vera Lynn was due to sing there, but our leave was cancelled so we couldn't go.

One evening, Philip enjoyed his gin a bit too much and became very agitated and impossible to calm down. Eventually, we had to leave him in Piccadilly. He told us later, after profuse apologies for his unpleasant behaviour, that he had spent the rest of the night climbing lampposts! He hated the taste of gin after that and never touched another drop in his life; beer and the occasional whisky became his tipples of choice.

How do I know this? Can't you guess?

After several dates, Philip and I became close. He was nothing like Tam; in fact, he was the total opposite in almost every way. No one could ever replace Tam in my heart, but Philip was tall and slim, and very good looking. He was also a couple of years younger than me, which made him half Tam's age, but I liked him and his company very much. Just like Tam, he was a decent and clever man.

Philip was doing his officer training at Woolwich, which he was enjoying a lot. We spent as much time together as possible, but it wasn't easy to get leave at the same time. We usually met up in London, which was easy for both of us to get to.

A little while later, Philip told me that he was being sent overseas, but wasn't allowed to talk about where he was going. But I guessed from the work I was doing at Bletchley that his destination would be India and my heart sank; the climate and conditions would not suit him at all. Having received hundreds of messages from that part of the world, I knew that we had a major offensive looming. Philip would be fighting the Japanese and we had heard their treatment of prisoners of war was appalling. I don't think Philip knew as much as I did, or if he did, he never mentioned it.

Philip was due to leave soon for Catterick Camp, and I knew I wouldn't see him again before his departure overseas. We embraced for the final time and he left me feeling sad. Even though I hadn't been looking for any romantic involvement after Tam, I was slowly falling in love with Philip and believed he felt the same way about me. I was still hurt and bruised from the shock of losing dear Tam, and now I might lose Philip as well. But he was special to me and no one else would take his place while he was away.

After Philip left, Eva tried to cheer me up by inviting me to her family home again, but I didn't take any leave for many months, so it was a long time before I saw her again. Eva never gave up, though, and eventually she persuaded me to meet up with her in London.

Eva and I met in Piccadilly for coffee and had a good catch up. Her romance with Gerry was going steadily and she told me that he had invited her to America when the war was over. I said that I had only received one letter from Philip and was rather disappointed that it had been short and factual. No statements of love and affection. Eva smiled and said that was typical of Philip and he would never change. Even though she knew he was very fond of me, it was just his way, she explained.

We decided to take the Tube to Oxford Street for some shopping; we were both short of clothes and had a little money saved. Just as we walked out of Bond Street Station, there was a huge explosion; a massive bomb had landed nearby and the fierce blast of burning air blew us back into the Tube station.

We were both forced up against the station wall and I must have passed out for a few moments. Eva was shaking my shoulder when I opened my eyes and sat up. Miraculously, we were both just dazed and bruised, but not seriously harmed.

Within minutes, we heard the urgent sirens, and ambulances raced towards Oxford Street. We left the station and walked towards Marble Arch, witnessing the terrible devastation to the shops and nearby buildings. The ambulance crews were helping those who were seriously wounded and we were sad to see dozens of dead bodies in the street, seemingly scattered randomly over the area.

I couldn't believe that a bomb, or even several of them, could cause such damage. People were saying it was a Buzz Bomb, so named because it made a buzzing noise when it was flying, and when this stopped, it was time to take cover. Eva and I, of course, had been inside the station at the time, so had had no warning. I had heard of these bombs before, but knew them as V2 rockets or doodlebugs.

Neither of us had ever been so close to such a devastating weapon before and it was a horrible experience. Eva and I spoke to one of the ambulance men to ask what we could do to help, and he told us politely but firmly that they needed space to tend to the injured and we should turn around towards Oxford Circus and follow the crowds out of danger. Eva and I decided then to make our separate ways back home.

Two images will stay in my mind of that day. The first is of piles of nude dummies lying in the middle of Oxford Street. The second is of huge Christmas trees, which had been blasted out of Selfridges, lying alongside them.

I was sent back to Bletchley Park from Stanmore. The German machines had become much more sophisticated and our Bombes couldn't decode the messages any longer. The Lorenz Cipher System used a second machine and all messages were coded twice, so for a long time, we were unable to decipher anything. Then our scientists developed Colossus machines and I worked with them at Bletchley. They too were much more sophisticated than the Bombes, but were prone to breaking down and seemed to need constant maintenance. Luckily, a mark two machine was developed which was far superior, but still we worked for months and made no progress at all.

And then we had a stroke of luck.

It appeared that two German operators had been working on decoding a message, but made a huge miscalculation when they broke procedure. They failed to re-code the message with both machines, and the upshot was that we received two separate wordings with different codes. By a process of elimination, we were able to understand both codes.

After our breakthrough, the Germans' machines were useless, although they didn't know it. We were able to read all their messages from land and sea. Fortunately, this happened just before D-Day so we were very well prepared. Indeed, we were told that without our good work, many more lives would have been lost and the success of the whole operation would have been in question.

I was still working with the Colossus machine at Bletchley Park when Mountbatten came to congratulate us. He said that our brilliant work had shortened the war and that the end was now in sight. Mountbatten was our ultimate boss, but this was the only time I saw him.

From the signals I'd received in the section where I now worked, I had clear information that he'd travelled to Japan during the war, disguised as a Japanese officer. This story might sound unbelievable, but I know what I heard and saw. Of course, I can't tell you anything else because I have signed the Official Secrets Act!

Part Four

The Forgotten Army

CHAPTER 17

Philip

I heard the voice from many miles away, at one time loud and clear, then echoing and coming closer, and then moving away again. It was insistent; I tried to hear what it was saying, but at the same time, I didn't want to. The truth was that I wanted to stay here and die if necessary; I was warm and comfortable as if I was still in my mother's womb. However, a muscular hand was gripping my shoulder hard and shaking me vigorously.

"Leave me alone!" I wanted to say this, but the words would not come. I had no idea what I was doing here and no longer cared. I was asleep anyway so why couldn't I just stay asleep? No one had the right to wake me and take me away from this deep comfort. I was back in my mother's care. I was warm and nourished in the arms of Morpheus, gentle as an angel's wings and soft as clouds. The colours were magnificent and I hoped this happy state would go on for ever.

But this was more than sleep; it was a deeply unconscious state.

I had been dreaming of terrifying wars from long ago. For some reason, I was in the centre of a fierce battle for control of a narrow pass. We faced innumerable foes, and the more we stabbed with our spears, the more came to fill the gaps. How much longer could we hold out? We were all tiring, but if we stopped for a rest, we would be dead in moments. So, we pushed and stabbed and pushed and stabbed while our leaders were shouting at us to hold our ground and keep going.

My body was so tired and my arms were beginning to disobey my brain, which was urging them to keep pushing. The effort to raise them was almost too much, but somehow, I kept going. Then someone grabbed me from behind and dragged me backwards.

I wasn't too worried as I knew I was being taken back to safety, away from the fighting zone. Whoever had grabbed me carried me to a nearby cave, laid me down on soft sand and ordered me to rest. Immediately, I drifted into a deep sleep, but what seemed like moments later, I was shaken awake, given some water to drink and some welcome bread.

I looked up and saw that the sun had moved across the sky. Unbeknown to me, I had been asleep for several hours. I was led to a hot pool nearby where I bathed my bloody body and soothed my wounds. The heat of the water was almost unbearably wonderful and my aching body was eased immediately. Then I was hauled out, dried and taken back to the narrow part of the pass. I was back in the centre of the action until my body wore down once more.

And then the soft and beautiful colours came back and filled my mind. I heard wonderful music and drifted upwards on swelling clouds. I wanted this enlightened happy state to go on for ever, but it was not to be.

Slowly, the sky darkened and huge black clouds filled it. I tried to will the colours and lovely feelings back, but instead, fierce winds roared across the land and bright flashes of lightning filled my vision. And then the rain came and soaked the earth and everything on it.

The lightning changed colour to a fierce red, then to deep crimson. It flashed from one colour to another, and then all colours at once. Thunder filled the air with a deep lion-like roar and the world began its descent into black hell. Fierce dragons were coming towards me and there was no escape. A terribly animated version of Munch's painting *the Scream* filled my vision and fearsome sounds assaulted my ears. I screamed and screamed in dread and anguish.

And now, when I was finally back in a deep sleep, someone was trying to shake me out of it. The strong hand was insistent. The pain became intense and I opened an eye. I wanted to go back to sleep, but the voice was getting louder in my ear.

"Wake up, sir, wake up! We've had a direct hit. Wake up!"

I opened one eye, tried to open the other and failed. My eyelid was stuck. I wanted to tell the voice to go away and leave me in peace, but the next few words made my body jerk with alarm.

"Half the men are dead, sir!"

The voice and strong hand belonged to Sergeant Dobie. It was the same voice that a few hours earlier had said to me, "Sir, you have had no rest for nine days and nights now. I will look after our men tonight, sir, and you will sleep."

He'd put his heavy hand on to my shoulder and led me to my tent, making sure I was lying on my camp bed before he left. I was too tired to protest, or even feel guilty, and remembered nothing but dreams until he shook me awake.

"What? What did you say?" I shouted.

"I said that we've had a direct hit from the Jap guns and half the men are dead or badly wounded."

My name is Philip Masterson and I was born in India in 1923. I am now twenty years old and a Lieutenant in the Royal Artillery. The last few years from the end of my schooling to my arrival in India seem to have been completed in a rush; I left Wellington

College early to join the Army to fight for my country.

Ten years earlier, I had been taking my Common Entrance exam at prep school when I was called into the headmaster's office to be told my father, Herbert, had died. He had only just passed his sixtieth birthday. I was thirteen years old and the news hit me like an express train. I was devastated.

I was taken back home to see my mother and sisters. Like many boys, I had hero worshipped my father, who had served with great distinction in the Indian Army in the Supply and Transport Corps, and in Mesopotamia and South Africa. The Army fought to protect northern India from Afghanistan and formed a first line of defence against the ever-present threat of Russian invasion.

When my father retired, he came back to England to join us where we had settled near Felixstowe in Suffolk. He was such a gentle and loving man with unshakeable Christian principles who had a natural affinity with all animals – he could train even the most stubborn Bull Terrier. But his quiet and mild manner masked a determined nature; he was hugely respected by his men and was not to be underestimated by anyone.

Herbert met my mother, Amelia, in India when she travelled there alone from England to nurse her brother Eddie back to full health after he was seriously wounded in Mesopotamia. My mother's extraordinary solo journey in the middle of World War I gave her an almost celebrity status amongst the northern Indian community. My father had rescued Eddie and many of his fellow soldiers who had been wounded at the terrible battle of Kut in Mesopotamia, where the British Indian Army had been trapped by the Ottoman Army in a bend of the River Tigris (as described in the book *From Eden to Babylon*).

The men had been starved into submission over a five-month period and only the most seriously wounded were released, the remainder being force-marched one thousand miles north into Anatolia where they became slaves of the Ottomans, forced to tunnel through mountains on poor rations while staying in basic accommodation. Rarely had soldiers been so brutally treated by their captors and only a third of them made it back to their homes, and those who did had been changed forever. The enormity of these war crimes was only exceeded by the atrocities committed by the Japanese in World War II some twenty years later, but sadly, no one stood trial for them.

The seriously wounded released by the victorious Ottomans were allowed to travel by ship and barge down the River Tigris to Basra. Many did not survive the terrible five-day journey as they received no care, treatment or medicines and were exposed to the extreme weather. Herbert and his men took the half-dead survivors off the barge in Basra and put them on a steamship to Bombay. He then took them by train to a sanatorium in Simla in the north of the country, a journey of one thousand miles, where they were well cared for.

Amelia's brother Eddie was one of the seriously wounded men who survived the journey to Simla. There, on Herbert's advice, he wrote to his sister in England to let her know of his plight, and so began her courageous solo journey into a hostile and terrifying world.

Amelia and Herbert were married in Murree, northern India, in 1920 and were blessed with three children shortly afterwards: Eva in 1921, Rosa in 1922, and I arrived in 1923. My health suffered in the harsh climate and doctors advised that white-skinned children should spend no more than three years in India, so my mother took me and my two older sisters back to England and we settled near Felixstowe. Father had a few more years' service in India to complete before re-joining his family in England.

While my mother was alone, I had a list of daily duties, which became rather repetitive and boring. To keep myself interested in these tasks, I designed and built a Meccano vehicle for carrying the coal into the house. Occasionally, we all played together, my sisters and I, but I missed male company. But on the whole, we had a happy and carefree childhood. I particularly enjoyed the usual boyhood adventures in the countryside and a daily swim in the sea.

One day, however, I nearly drowned when I was dragged out by a strong tide. I felt confident in the water as I'd studied the tide tables and the sun and moon's gravitational forces, so I was completely surprised by the power of the water on that day. As I was pulled a couple of miles out, the shoreline faded into the distance. Then the force subsided and I was able to tread water for several hours, slowly making my way back to land. Darkness had fallen by the time I got home to an extremely worried mother.

My clearest memories are of the happiest of times when my father Herbert came home from India. At last I had some male company. He taught me carpentry skills and we spent hours building furniture and labour-saving gadgets for Mother and the family.

When Herbert died, it was a terrible shock to all of us, and it was no surprise when a letter arrived from my school to tell me that I had failed my Common Entrance exam. Under the circumstances, though, I was allowed to retake it, and fortunately I passed. My father's death meant I received a bursary to board at Wellington College, a military school, so my mother, who was surviving on a small part of Herbert's pension, only had to pay £5 a year for my education there.

CHAPTER 18

A Return to India

After a difficult start, I soon fell into the routine at Wellington. I did quite well in lessons and sports, but I was aware that I was not an outstanding academic student. I made many friends, some of whom I kept in touch with for years, and I was extremely proud to be a pupil at the school. Its motto *Heroum Filii*, Sons of Heroes, and religious instruction motivated and directed my spirit. I learned the meaning of loyalty, commitment and faithfulness, and determined to apply these principles throughout my life.

Many of the masters, or ushers as we called them, had served in World War I, some in the Afghan wars, and a few in the Boer war of some forty years before. Most of us went on to join the Officer Training Corps, which laid the foundation for my military career.

We were mainly sheltered from the early part of World War II, but whenever we heard the air-raid sirens, we were led to one of the bunkers just outside the school gates. One night, a solo German bomber released its heavy load directly above us, and unfortunately it hit the headmaster's house, killing him instantly. The loss of 'Bobby' Longden had a depressing effect on all the boys and masters as he was a great human being who'd had a profoundly positive influence on our lives. Tragically, he was only thirty-six years old.

After leaving Wellington, I started officer training at Woolwich and Catterick and prepared to join the Royal Artillery. On my days off, I would join my friends for lively nights out in London, which led to me meeting up with my sister, Eva, for an evening in the American Bar at the Savoy.

When I arrived, the bar was heaving with people, mostly servicemen and women who were determined to enjoy every moment of their lives, which might easily be cut short. When the air-raid sirens started their wailing, no one changed their step; they just carried on partying. I even heard one man say, "Eat, drink and be merry, for tomorrow we die."

I spotted Eva seated at a table on the other side of the bar, holding on to the arm of an American airman, talking to him in her usual animated way. Opposite them sat a young woman I didn't recognise. Dressed in the uniform of the Wrens, she looked lovely.

I joined them and was introduced to Eva's companions. The young woman was Eva's friend from her days at domestic science college in Torquay, and her name was Isla Smythson. The American airman was called Gerry, and I could see immediately that he and Eva were developing feelings for each other.

After a couple of drinks, we moved to the ballroom for dancing to a live American band I had never heard of. The man at the front of the stage was playing the most beautiful jazz trumpet while a woman in evening dress sang, her soulful voice a joy to hear. Behind them, the band members kept a hypnotic rhythm going. Even though I am no dancer, I couldn't help moving and swaying to the sounds.

However, the highlight of the evening was meeting Isla. After that, we got together on many occasions during my time at Woolwich and inevitably grew close. When I was ordered abroad to serve in India, she and I had a very sad parting. I wasn't allowed to tell her where I was going, but I think she knew anyway; her work gave her access to confidential information which she was not allowed to discuss with anyone.

I joined a troop ship from Southampton to Calcutta for an uneventful but uncomfortable trip. There were just too many people on board. As soon as I stepped off the ship, though, I was back in the land of my birth. Although I'd left many years before, I recognised the place: the peculiar warm-scented spicy smells; the intense heat and dust; the hustle and bustle; and above all, the friendly people in their multi-coloured clothes. Huge crowds thronged around me and the buzzing of hundreds of voices filled my ears. I loved the extraordinary red-coloured buildings reflecting the changing light and shade, the sense of history. Back in my first home, I was happy to be here.

Our training was designed to simulate jungle fighting against the Japanese, and it was – and had to be – incredibly tough. So far, the Japanese had the upper hand in Burma and had pushed our Allied Army out of the country. But our leaders believed that with more intense and appropriate training, we could beat them.

We had to learn to survive the monsoon season and the geographical obstacles of the region. Above all, we had to conquer our fears and develop a positive and determined nature. Several men did not thrive in this environment and three of my friends were assigned admin duties.

We learnt to parachute from a plane, practising every day. We stripped down and set up artillery guns and learnt all the different ways to transport them. Aiming and firing our guns at targets sometimes miles away, we discovered how to make small adjustments for movement. Long day and night marches in all weathers honed our resilience, and we were mock attacked frequently without notice by men dressed as Japanese soldiers. We became skilled in radio communications on the ground and in the air.

On one occasion, I was leading a group of six men. Our mission was to locate a target, in this case an old lorry, and then find a suitable place to set up our guns and blow it to bits. We were competing against four other teams.

I sent two men to climb up the highest hill with a good pair of binoculars and a radio. After a couple of hours, they buzzed and gave me the map reference of the lorry. I then looked for a high position to set up our gun, a mountain howitzer, and found a hill on the map which looked suitable. We stripped down the gun and used six mules to carry the parts up to the top. Unfortunately, the rain was drilling down, which made the task difficult and miserable.

Once we arrived at the top of the hill, we took minutes to reassemble the gun and load it. We had been given limited ammunition and time for the task, just two days, so we had to be quick and accurate.

Just before we were ready to fire, I heard a blast to my left and saw a puff of smoke drifting upwards. It looked like one of the rival teams was ahead of us, but I was determined to win this and assure my passage to Burma.

The shot had missed, but not by much, and I urged my team to get ready to fire, hopefully with deadly accuracy. We overshot by about a hundred yards, so after readjusting the angles, I yelled at them to reload quickly and fire before the others did. This time, the lorry disintegrated in a cloud of smoke and the explosion was massive. I was delighted and praised my team for their good work.

When we regrouped, our Indian verifiers informed us that my team had hit the target, but so had another team at exactly the same time. I was, of course, extremely disappointed that we hadn't won the contest outright and asked the verifiers how they had come to this conclusion. Apparently, they were taking the other team, who had claimed they had hit the lorry, at their word, so I asked to visit the site with the verifiers.

After searching for a few moments, we found a blackened crater a few yards to the right of the target, and it didn't take the verifiers long to confirm that the other team had missed after all. My team was the undisputed winner of the exercise and our place in the Burma expedition was confirmed.

However, nothing could have prepared us for the horrors to come.

After several more weeks of training, we were looking forward to getting on with the task of ridding Burma of the enemy. We loaded several Dakotas, kindly provided by our American friends, with our weaponry and equipment.

After a flight of a couple of hours which was bumpy but uneventful, we landed in the city of Dimapur. This was actually in Nagaland, which is a state of India, and not Burma at all, although the border was not too far away. Dimapur was in chaos with no one sure of what was happening. There was an absence of command and organisation, and we were sent to the wrong camp several times.

Our leaders were expecting an attack by the Japanese, who were desperate to get their hands on our supplies as they hadn't brought enough food or weaponry with them. Our supply stores at Dimapur occupied a vast area, eleven miles long and one mile wide, so it would certainly be a huge prize for the Japanese if they could break through.

Hundreds of Japanese soldiers had crossed the Irrawaddy and Chindwin Rivers and were moving with great speed through Burma, threatening to invade India. Our Army had been forced to retreat over the past two years as the Japanese had gained the upper hand. There was now a determination to stop them, and enormous resources of men and equipment were being made available to achieve this.

We had a huge Army at Imphal in the almost inaccessible hilly country south of us, and their only connection to our main stores and railway at Dimapur was by a steep and twisty road north, some one hundred and twenty miles away. Approximately halfway along this dangerous road was a small town called Kohima. The road twisted around, through and above this town, and we understood that it was vital to stop the Japanese here. Kohima was situated on a ridge of hills rising to around five thousand feet, surrounded by higher mountains. The terrain was steep and wooded – the most inhospitable place to defend. But there was no other way to get to our forces at Imphal, who were now under attack. If we lost Kohima, they would be cut off. If the Japanese succeeded in overcoming Dimapur, the road to India would then be open to them and the British Empire would be seriously threatened.

While in Dimapur waiting for our orders, I had time to write letters to my mother and Isla. We had to be careful not to give away any details at all about our situation and our letters were heavily censored; we could only say we were well and safe, and hope all was good at home. I am glad I took this opportunity to write, though, as I would have no time in the coming weeks.

Then I started dreaming about the future. If I survived this war – indeed, if any of us did – would Isla and I be together? Would we get married and have children? I wondered what I would do for a living when the war was over – assuming we had won it and were able to make our own decisions.

It seemed that the tide was turning in the Allies' favour, although we still had a herculean job to do. Could I stay in the Army? I would like to, but I also wanted a change of direction. I had always been fascinated with aircraft. A career in design or manufacturing flying machines would be my dream. I also liked working with my hands, thanks to the strong direction of my father, and had become quite a proficient carpenter and metal worker.

We spent a couple of days preparing our guns, ammunition and transport, and then received our orders to drive to Kohima. I didn't know why we were carrying so much ammunition: we had twenty-five lorry loads, but as it happened, we would need even more. Loads more.

Our journey was difficult. We were navigating the impossibly steep roads in the heaviest rain I had ever seen, and this was before the monsoon season had officially started. The trees grew thickly all over the slopes and along both sides of the road. I couldn't get over the greenness of the land, which was constantly soaked from either the rains or the intensely hot, steamy air.

How on earth could an army move or fight through this terrain? On one occasion, a gun carriage skidded off the road into a ditch and it took hours of back-breaking work to push it out again. Then we faced a road blockage after a steep earth bank collapsed. Again, it took dozens of men hours to dig through it.

Eventually, we took a road to the right up the side of a huge mountain called Puliebadze. We stopped a little way up near a spur of the mountain for a few hours while our Colonel carried out a recce.

He returned and informed us that he had selected a flat piece of land near a small village higher up on a ridge overlooking Kohima, about two miles away from the village. We drove up there and saw that it was an excellent place to view the hills, but as it was not the highest land, it could be overlooked, particularly from Puliebadze above us. Despite the drawbacks, the Colonel decided that our Army would camp at this place, which was near to a village called Jotsoma.

We were expecting the Japanese to arrive any day and would have an extremely hard job to hold them back. Privately, we talked about what they would do to us if we were captured by them as we had heard terrible stories of their treatment of our people.

They were extremely cruel to the men, women and children they had captured after the fall of Singapore and Hong Kong. Many had been bayoneted by them.

We also knew the Japanese were renowned as fierce warriors who had no care for their own safety and would fight to the death. Their determination to defeat the enemy and bring pride to their families, the Japanese nation and their emperor was their driving force. If they lost their lives in their endeavour, they believed they would gain immortal praise.

This made them an extremely dangerous enemy. To our minds, they had none of our values or character, to put it mildly. But our leaders were adamant that they were only men; they were not invincible and we could defeat them. Our training had given us a positive attitude; even though the Japanese had already pushed the Allies out of Burma, we were determined to fight back and regain the country.

We had been well-trained in India and our gun teams quickly went to work. I was feeling nervous leading a team of twenty men in my first real action, so I gave orders to my Sergeant who relayed them to the men and reported back when the job was complete. As is the army custom, he always called me sir, even though I was half his age. If he believed

I was giving the wrong orders, he would whisper a timely suggestion out of earshot of the men, and I would alter the order accordingly.

This extraordinary man's name was Sergeant Dobie. Little did I know just how much I would come to rely on him.

CHAPTER 19

A Journey into Hell

Dobie – I never knew his Christian name – had fought in Palestine in World War I as a young Corporal. In quieter moments, he would tell us stories of his incredible adventures under General Allenby, who all the men had had great respect for. Dobie told us Allenby's nickname had been Bloody Bull, although no one dared to call him that to his face.

Unfortunately for the men, Allenby overheard a radio message saying, "Bloody Bull is coming". As luck would have it, though, when Allenby asked what this meant, a quick-thinking soldier was on hand with the perfect response.

"Don't worry, sir," he said, "it's only a small agricultural issue."

Dobie had been at the final battle of Megiddo when the Turks were routed by the combined Allied forces of infantry, cavalry, destroyers in the nearby Mediterranean, aeroplanes from the newly formed RAF and artillery. This was where the man who was alongside me in the difficult conditions of India had gained his early experience, and I was so glad of his expertise.

We dug our gun pits into the side of the hill near Jotsoma, just below the top, and lowered the guns into place. Lining up twelve guns, we awaited radio orders from the centre of action to delay or destroy attacking forces, bunkers or artillery positions. I oversaw three of the guns with my team.

We set up our camp in a sheltered position and dug out our latrines some way apart. The streams which trickled down the mountain gave us a good water supply, unlike our infantry two miles away on the hills of Kohima who we heard were constantly struggling to find enough water. We were also well supplied with food and had some good cooks from our Indian regiments. For breakfast each morning, we were spoiled with plenty of hot tea, along with porridge, sausages, bacon and biscuits, all served in dented metal containers. Once again, we were luckier than our friends across the valley.

On our first morning in camp, I had a good look at the land below us through my binoculars. I looked at the huge mountain behind us, and then moved my sight slowly to my left, towards the east. The next spur came into view, and then I saw the road to Imphal about two miles away. That was the direction the enemy was coming from, and I saw an endless line of them moving towards us. Aiming my binoculars further left towards the north, I saw several hills and ridges, each of which had been given a nickname by us. This was where our defending Army was positioned.

In the next few days, we would get to know each area intimately and would sometimes take instruction by nickname rather than grid reference, but I preferred to know exactly where our fire was needed so that there could be no misunderstanding. On one occasion, we'd hit our own men and we couldn't risk repeating this.

As I scanned the land features, I knew that the Allies held all of them except the first hill on the far side of the road. The Japanese were setting up their artillery there and it was our job to displace them. The Allied forces were defending the adjacent few hills, but our men were hopelessly outnumbered.

The first place to come under fire had been nicknamed Jail Hill. I rested my binoculars on the old prison building and saw it was already a wreck.

As I moved my binoculars to view the far side of the hills where our troops were, the land fell away in a series of tiers. I could see the tennis court and, lower down, the bungalow of the District Commissioner, which would see some of the fiercest fighting of the war.

The road continued around the bungalow and took a sharp left. Just beyond was the town of Kohima, and then the Naga village which was shortly to become occupied by the Japanese. The Nagas were the indigenous people of the land and were extremely helpful to our Army. If I listened carefully, I could hear the cocks crowing from the village – faintly.

Looking a few miles beyond the village, I saw a line of six elephants walking towards Kohima. I assumed that the Japanese were carrying heavy guns to new positions and I reported this immediately to my Senior Officer. I then retraced my line of sight. I thought I saw movement just outside the Naga village and refocused the lens; yes, it looked as if a crowd of ants was moving forward with purpose, but I realised that these were men. These were the enemy.

As I rechecked the view of the area, I saw more and more men, and it became apparent that our position was being surrounded with incredible speed. Our camps in the hills of Kohima would soon be attacked from all sides. The Japanese were moving up the mountain towards us, making a path around us to the north, meaning that they would reach the road to Dimapur within hours and we would be cut off. The Japanese would overrun the garrison and capture our stores and airfield.

I was extremely worried for the men already trapped, who would be struggling for survival. For one moment, I imagined the Japanese attacking our position on the hill near Jotsoma and capturing our guns. In that event, there would be no artillery support for our men. Would we be killed or captured? Most men hoped for a swift end as captivity was unthinkable.

One thing was certain: we were all going to have to fight for our lives and defend our precarious positions. I ordered my men to fire, reload and fire again. The incredible noise blasted our senses and filled our heads and bodies – no wonder retired artillerymen over the centuries have suffered from acute deafness – and the smoke billowed in thick smelly clouds around us and into the valley.

When the orders with the targets came through each morning by radio from the Kohima hills, we would carefully line up the guns to precise angles. I would carry out final checks to make sure the angles were correct, and every few minutes, when a gun ceased firing, I was able to make tiny adjustments as necessary. It wasn't unusual for each gun to fire four to five hundred rounds every day, and we often carried on through the night, the shots sparking like little lightning flashes in the sky.

The huge supply of ammunition we had carried into the hills soon ran low, and then threatened to run out. We called for more supplies and air drops of ammunition were made to us just in time.

It was exhausting work. The heat from the guns almost cooked us, and together with the muggy temperature, it had drained us completely by the end of the day, but we kept on firing. When the dreadful monsoon rains came, the guns created clouds of steam, and dirty rivulets of sweat ran down our bodies. The local biting insects had a field day.

Then the day came when I was ordered to report to Major Yeoman who was based on Garrison Hill, roughly in the centre of the Kohima range across the valley. He would radio us several times a day to give us grid references and pass on all the information we needed to blast away at the attacking Japanese. The purpose of my visit was to see the lie of the land and the Japanese positions so that my men could fire more accurately and effectively.

I was to walk to the meeting, a journey of around two miles across difficult terrain, and I was pleased to be ordered to take Sergeant Dobie with me rather than going on my own. The journey would be extremely difficult and dangerous and the chances of us surviving were low, but we had to risk it.

We left in the early hours while it was still dark. It was already raining and the going was slippery. We had to walk down our spur to the valley below; we knew there was no enemy presence there, yet. The slope was almost vertical and thickly wooded, and at times we would skid down and have to aim for a tree to stop our slide. On one occasion, I was falling forwards so fast, I couldn't stop myself until I crashed into my long-suffering sergeant. As ever, he took the battering with good grace.

When we started our upward climb, I felt a heavy force on the top of my back as my sergeant pushed me down. As I fell forward, Dobie's left hand covered my face to prevent me making any sounds. He had seen something.

I moved my head up slowly and looked through the gloomy morning air. Shadowy figures were moving across our position. Dobie whispered in my ear that a line of enemy soldiers was going from left to right about twenty yards ahead of us. We stayed on the ground, hardly daring to breathe in case they heard us.

I remained stock-still, even though the damp from the earth was drenching my uniform through to my skin. Certain the enemy would hear my thumping heart, I watched them moving across. One man shot a glance in our direction. Had he seen us? I was absolutely terrified and feared the worst. Later, Dobie confessed that he'd felt just the same. All men did, he said, and those who claimed they didn't were bloody liars.

Eventually, the Japanese disappeared from view, but we kept still for many more minutes. Finally, Dobie raised his head very slowly. When he was convinced that all the soldiers had gone, he told me to look around to confirm his belief. I saw no one.

When I got up, my body hurt terribly and I almost cried out. My muscles had stiffened after the tough journey. The damp of the ground hadn't helped and the rain was falling more heavily now. Dobie whispered that the monsoon had started early this year. Just our luck!

As we walked towards the slope of the hill, clods of earth shot up into our faces and a deafening rat-a-tat shocked us out of our reverie. A horrible zipping and cracking noise ripped up the earth in front of us, getting dangerously close. We slammed our bodies back into the muddy ground; once again, I was terrified and thought that we were dead men. I was bitterly disappointed that it should all end now after I had come so far. My guts felt watery and my chest hurt as I struggled to breathe. I stiffened in preparation for my skin and bones to be ripped apart by the bullets. My hands shook and my whole body was quivering uncontrollably.

"Skid backwards and keep your head down," Dobie told me in a hoarse whisper. I slithered backwards as fast as possible; I could have outpaced a large snake.

"See where it's coming from. Must be a Sten gun."

We both peered into the undergrowth, but couldn't see the source of the danger. We kept moving backwards, and then Dobie whispered to me to lie still. This was the first time I had been in close action and I was pleased to have him with me for much-needed support. Staring time and time again into the undergrowth and trees to catch sight of our shooter, we saw nothing.

After about an hour, we stood up slowly and walked along a route several degrees to the right. I was so grateful to have been spared, but we never did find out where the bullets had been coming from. Sometimes I have moments, even years later, of wondering what the hell had happened. Was this a lone gunman who tried to kill us before being called back to the main body of men? Or was someone firing into the mist just to empty his gun?

We approached the steeper part of the hill and crawled up the slope. At last, the ground evened out and we saw our men ahead. Now we were entering the most dangerous part of our mission – we might be mistaken for enemy soldiers.

Dobie called out, "We are two British soldiers from Jotsoma."

Shots were fired over our heads and the whistling sounds of bullets were alarmingly close. I held my breath.

Dobie raised his head again. "We are here to meet Major Yeoman," he stated clearly.

We were greatly relieved when a voice with a strong Kentish accent yelled back, "Well, why the fuck didn't you say that?"

Before long, we were safely ensconced in a trench with a group of our men, who asked us about our mission. All the while, the noise around us was deafening and relentless, but I was greatly relieved to be with our own and silently thanked Our Saviour for sparing Dobie and me this time.

The men told us that they were so suspicious of everyone because some Japanese spoke perfect English. They had been known to rush towards Allied positions, yelling, "Quick, the Japs are after us! Let us through!" On one occasion, two of our men had been shot before the others realised they'd been tricked and took defensive action. It was no wonder they remained cautious, even when they heard voices speaking their own language.

One of the men told us that he'd been advancing forward one time when he and his companions had found the body of a British soldier tied to a tree. The Japanese had used him for bayonet practice. I could not believe that their soldiers could be so viciously brutal, while starting to understand the type of enemy we were up against.

The men all wanted to know what was happening in Jotsoma and whether a relief force was on its way. We were unable to tell them as we hadn't been informed ourselves. I felt desperately sorry for them. They had held out under extremely difficult circumstances against vast numbers of fanatical soldiers and had been promised relief many times, but no forces had materialised. The artillery bombardment around us was nonstop; it reminded us that our men were hopelessly outnumbered by the enemy.

We were given a mug of hot tea each, which was extremely welcome, but we had to drink it quickly as we didn't want to keep the Major waiting. We didn't realise until later that all drinks in this camp were rationed due to the shortage of water and these men had generously given us some of their limited supply.

We were escorted by a couple of the men up the last two hundred yards or so to meet the Major. It was tough climbing the slippery slope and I wondered how they could fight in such terrible conditions. The sound of guns and grenades exploding was constant and we ducked instinctively as the artillery shells roared past us and exploded further up the hill.

I was horrified to see the state of the soldiers. They were desperately tired, having had few opportunities to sleep for more than a few minutes. A longer sleep meant almost certain death. Their clothes were ragged, covering emaciated frames; they reminded me of the scarecrows I used to see on the flat farmlands of my home in the East of England. The men here were desperately short of food and water, but above all, they needed rest. They didn't know when the next shell would blast them apart or the next bayonet charge would end their existence.

"When we die, sir, is that the end or do we go on?" This poignant question had been asked by a young private of his officer, the men with us told Dobie and me.

The bombardment had blasted the leaves and branches of the trees away, leaving rough stumps. Many trees around the area were draped in different coloured parachute cloth. Each parachute represented goods thrown out of aeroplane doors – food, water and ammunition – as essential supplies had been dropped for our men from Dakotas over the past few days. The parachutes were ragged and torn, dripping from the heavy rain and billowing in the wind, adding to the sense of terrible devastation all around us. Unfortunately, many had drifted into enemy-occupied areas, and the Japanese were now benefitting from these supplies. Apparently, they had come to call them 'Churchill's rations'.

On one occasion, there had been a huge mix up when we at Jotsoma had received supplies desperately needed by those at Kohima, and they'd received our shells. Luckily, that only happened once. Sometimes the parachutes failed to open, and a box of shells had crashed into some men stationed just above our guns. One had suffered a broken arm. Many brave airmen risked their lives getting supplies to us all, often flying too low, and one had tragically crashed into the mountain above us. The enemy didn't receive supplies from their own people and often had to steal from the local villagers or indeed from us.

I was horrified at the demoralising devastation and found it hard to believe that these men had survived for so long, although, of course, many hadn't. All around us were limbs ripped from men's bodies by the force of hundreds of explosions. There were torn-open jerrycans and hundreds of unidentified metal parts; there were craters, shells and every kind of debris, all encircled by a miasma of flies and mosquitoes. Behind us was a huge tented area where doctors were frantically attending to the wounded, all the while targeted by the mortars and artillery of the enemy. The scene reminded me of Dante's journey through hell in his *Divine Comedy*, but his vision was limited by comparison. Yet still our men fought and resisted.

CHAPTER 20

The Battle Intensifies

At last, we reached the HQ at the top of Garrison Hill. Major Yeoman was friendly, but businesslike; there was no time for pleasantries. We had urgent jobs and responsibilities to get back to.

He showed us a map of the hills his men were defending and highlighted the areas the Japanese had already taken. Then he took us to the far side of the hill so that we could look down over the tiers of the slope towards the District Commissioner's bungalow, which was now a complete wreck. There was a fierce battle taking place on the tennis court, which was no longer recognisable as such. The ground was rough and hard and had seen days of hand-to-hand fighting, shelling and mortaring. The enemy had come up from across the road and were bombarding our men over the narrow space, and they were fighting back with enormous courage.

I watched as the enemy lobbed grenades across the thirty yards or so of flat court towards where our men were dug in. One of our soldiers caught the Japanese grenades and threw them back. I had never seen such raw courage in action before.

"He used to play cricket for Cambridge, you know," Major Yeoman said. I didn't know whether to believe him or not.

Another man joined in the deadly game, catching the grenades one-handed and throwing them back. Then a third and fourth until the inevitable happened: one exploded the second it was caught, blowing the poor catcher to bits. But it didn't stop them.

The Japanese decided to charge and the defenders mowed them down. They charged again and fell, then a third and fourth time. Then our men charged, but we had to move on and didn't see the outcome.

The Major led us over to the far side of the hill so that we could see how the battle was unravelling there. To me, it all seemed hopeless; there were thousands of the enemy on all sides and only a few hundred of our incredibly brave men imprisoned in small areas of the hills which remained in our possession. The importance of the precision of our guns at Jotsoma was obvious, but the positions of both armies were changing in seconds. Our huge responsibility was to hit the right targets at the right time; Major Yeoman hardly needed to clarify this. That was, of course, as long as our men hadn't been overrun by the time we got back.

We moved further down the slope to get a closer look at the action. Dozens of our men had been horribly wounded and were being carried up the hill by courageous stretcher bearers to the medical station at the top. They were then taken down the far side to the makeshift tented hospital.

I witnessed extraordinary acts of bravery as one man ran towards an enemy machine gun post which was well-protected in a wooden bunker. Somehow, he survived by running under the line of fire, and then he lay below the bunker for a moment in relative safety. He drew pins from two grenades, waited a few seconds – far too long for my nerves – and lobbed them through the slit into the bunker. Ducking down once again while the explosion blasted out above him, he then stood up and looked into the gap to make sure the men were dead. He climbed into the bunker and carried out the heavy machine gun, holding it above his head to the roaring approval of his comrades. He then coolly walked back up the hill, still holding the gun, the men cheering wildly.

And then their mood changed.

"Watch out!"

"Get down, you bloody fool, for Christ's sake!"

We all groaned when he was mowed down by a dozen guns as the Japanese took their revenge. But there was no time to lose as a fierce fire fight had started; we were hustled back up the hill, crawling on our stomachs for safety. The Major wanted to talk to us about our strategy and said that he had arranged for much more detailed maps to be dropped to us by air. I was pleased as this would help enormously.

We had learned a huge amount from our short visit, but there was an urgency about the operation. We needed to return to get back to work as quickly as possible; the enemy could overrun our positions in hours.

As we made our way back down the hill, heading towards Jotsoma, the drumming rain had eased, replaced by extreme heat and steam. The flies and mosquitoes were buzzing around the dozens of dead Japanese soldiers a few yards ahead of us. The smell of their bloated bodies was horrible. Our men always tried hard to recover our dead and wounded comrades, often at a terrible cost, but the Japanese didn't seem to bother. Their soldiers' bodies were left to decompose.

The Major had given us a sketch map to guide us back while avoiding the enemy. I was eager to return to our guns at Jotsoma and put all we had learned into practice, hopefully becoming even more effective in stopping the Japanese attacks. Lost in thought as we made our way down the slope into the valley, I fervently hoped that we had seen our last Japanese soldier.

We had only been on our way for a few minutes when I heard a shot and a fierce buzzing sound, followed by a cry of agony from Dobie as he clutched his thigh and fell to the ground. I looked around, but saw no one.

"Look up – up there – sniper!" he yelled.

I still didn't see anything or anyone. Lying on his back on the ground, Dobie drew his pistol and fired twice. I heard a high-pitched scream. Looking up, I saw a Japanese soldier fall out of a tall tree a few yards away, but he didn't reach the ground. He was tied to the tree by a leg, so he was now hanging face down towards the earth. Dobie had made no mistake with his shot.

We watched as the sniper's hat fell to the ground. The menace of the snipers and the number of casualties caused by them was common knowledge, and we were pleased that there was now one less of these bloody devils.

Dobie was bleeding from his right thigh, but he was not badly wounded. He pulled down his trousers to expose the wound and I looked into my pack to find disinfectant and bandages. Together, we tied a rough bandage to stem the bleeding, while I tried to ignore his curses. I hoped that there were no more Japanese nearby, but we had to focus on the task in hand.

After a few minutes' rest, I helped Dobie to his feet and he tried to stand. When he complained that he had no feeling or control of his right leg, I knew that I would have to support him and get him back to base. With his arm around my shoulder, we both managed to stagger downhill until we reached the valley, thankfully without further incident.

I looked up at the steep hill covered in thick undergrowth ahead of us and felt deep despair. How on earth could I get this man up there? But there was no other option.

Dobie suggested we wait a few moments just to check we were alone, and then we slowly staggered towards our destination. As we moved forward, the undergrowth and roots tried hard to prevent our progress; within a few yards, I felt the sweat break out on my forehead, and then all over my head and down my back. We were both panting with the immense effort, and after a few minutes, Dobie ordered me to stop while we got our breathing under control. I looked back to see how far we had come and couldn't believe our lack of progress; our starting point was only yards away.

We carried on in this fashion for most of the afternoon, stopping for breaks and water until our bottle was dry. Dobie carried on stoically without complaining once. God, he was tough!

At last, we reached the foot of the hill leading to our camp, but I knew I could not get him up this almost vertical cliff. He knew it, too. I could hardly get up on my own, but I had to fetch help for him. I was reluctant to leave him, but he insisted that he would be OK. Climbing as quickly as I could, I called out our names and ranks just below the lip of the cliff.

A brown face looked down at me and I told the man our situation and that Dobie desperately needed water. Within minutes, four Punjabi soldiers climbed down to the sergeant, swinging on ropes tied to tree roots. It took them half an hour of huge effort to lift him back up and take him to the medical tent. After thanking them, I collapsed onto the ground with exhaustion.

I was tired, but relieved to have got back safely. However, there was no time to rest. I updated my men and other officers on the conversation I had had with the Major and we immediately agreed actions and priorities: we would start firing again almost nonstop. Hundreds of the enemy had climbed past us on the side of the mountain, and others had dug in high to our right, overlooking our position.

We turned two guns towards them and blasted away. Meanwhile, the Indian soldiers in Jotsoma above us moved forward to attack. Other Japanese soldiers had already climbed over the mountain with the aim of blocking the road to Dimapur. We hoped our forces would push them back and keep the road open.

My main focus was to support our men on the ridge of hills, in particular those on the tennis court some two miles away. As soon as the Japanese charged across, we fired and fired again, and managed to stop them. An overjoyed Major Yeoman radioed us to inform us that our aim was good enough to act in a Western!

We were called upon many times to frustrate the Japanese attacks, and then we were asked to redirect our aim to other areas where they were threatening our forces. We tried to blast the bunkers out of the ground; sometimes we were successful, but mostly they were dug in too deep.

We fired for the rest of the day and into the night. Still needing to knock out the Japanese artillery, we were continually changing our directions and angles. With the range of our guns, we could reach targets several miles away, so the shells needed a high trajectory without impeding their accuracy. I was amazed at how effective we became; it reminded me bizarrely of a time when I was watering the garden at home and was able to direct the stream from the hose exactly where I wanted it to fall.

Early the following morning, I was observing the Kohima hills through my binoculars, looking for any changes in the enemy's positions, when I heard a low roar coming from the left. I was thrilled to see one of our Hurribombers heading directly towards us, flying low through the valley. As this magnificent machine came closer, I could see the pilot quite clearly and I waved. He spotted me and returned the wave, and then pointed at a position just above us. As he swooped lower, he opened his window and threw a bag towards me. It landed about a hundred yards or so away from me. Before going to retrieve it, I checked that he was able to swoop over the mountain behind us safely and was greatly relieved when he did so.

I was delighted to see that the Major had made good on his promise: the bag contained a bundle of around a dozen maps of the area with much more detail than we had seen before. I looked up when the pilot was banking his plane to Dimapur in the north and waved my thanks to this brave man.

Meanwhile, the battle had intensified. The Japanese were swarming all over our positions with even greater determination, trying to overrun Jotsoma. We had no time to fight back, but there were two Indian regiments above us with rows of machine guns. They fired as the thousands of Japanese charged at us for hours at a time and their guns managed to keep the enemy at bay. There never seemed to be any real danger of us being overrun, but the enemy kept coming at us, despite the horrendous numbers being blown away.

Piles of bodies filled the lower slopes just below us. It seemed that the Japanese had an unending supply of suicide volunteers, but after several hours of constant charging, they finally gave up and retreated down the hill. Some groups climbed to their positions higher up and we shelled them non-stop as they joined their comrades. The Indian regiments had been bravely charging their position, but the Japanese had dug in well and their bunkers were almost impregnable. Our guns had little effect on them.

Despite our efforts and the bravery of our men, our Army was gradually retreating from the positions it had been holding at Kohima, and our men were forced from the hills one by one by sheer weight of enemy numbers until they regrouped on Garrison Hill. They were surrounded and trapped.

My best contribution would be to do my job to the utmost of my ability. I threw myself into the task and worked hour after hour with my men. The heat was overwhelming and sweat poured down our bodies before being washed away in the power of the rain. The guns often became overheated and steam blasted into our faces, but we carried on through the days and nights, making huge flashes of fire in the distance towards the range of hills around Kohima. Our men on Garrison Hill fought back against huge numbers of the enemy; mortars and shells lit the night sky every few minutes like massive fireworks. The noise was shattering and filled our heads, reverberating through our bodies and terrifying our souls.

The valleys echoed with this thunder and lightning bombardment. I made sure my men had regular breaks from their exhausting work, but I refused to stop myself. Dobie kindly brought me mugs of tea and tins of meat and beans, but I was only half aware of the food. He forced me to sit down a few paces away from the action, but after a few moments, I would be desperate to get back to my tasks. I owed it to the poor men I had met on those devastated hills and I was determined to do everything I could to reduce the impact of the Japanese attacks.

It seemed the Major never slept, either; he was constantly calling me on the radio with new targets or adjustments to existing directions. We fired and fired, and the days passed quickly, darkening into evenings before the black night closed in, only to be lit up again by our flashes of fire.

I was aware that it was Isla's birthday on 14 April, but I wasn't sure if the day had passed or if was still in the future. I asked Dobie and he told me I had missed the date, but I hadn't had the opportunity to write to her anyway. I would have felt guilty if I had taken the time off to do this.

I began to notice a recurring stabbing pain in my guts. I tried to ignore the discomfort it gave me and carry on, but the pain got worse and visits to the latrines confirmed that all was not well with my insides. My head was aching, but I forced my body to keep going. The work I was doing was too important to be left.

As I started to feel more and more tired and run down, I thought of Isla and wondered what she was doing. Did she miss me, or had she forgotten all about me? I knew she was doing important work with the Wrens, but not what this work entailed, only that it was highly secret and crucial for the success of our war. I wanted a life with Isla, and we both wanted children. We had decided on four and she even had names for them!

I thought about my poor mother at home in Felixstowe and my dear sisters, Eva teaching for the war effort and Rosa working as a Land Girl. They were both doing vital work – the extra food the Land Army produced kept many alive and healthy, and it was essential to cook the food properly as there was little being imported into Britain at this time.

I thought of my dear father who had died eight years earlier. I wished he was alive so that I could talk to him about my war and listen to his advice. He had been in many conflicts and great danger during his years in the Indian Army as a Lieutenant Colonel. He was taken from us far too early. I thought about his gentle manner and his love of animals and good people, and wondered how he had been able to generate great respect from his men with his soft approach. He rarely raised his voice or became angry, but still had a hugely successful career. I desperately wanted to emulate him, but I wasn't made of the same material.

I wondered, as all soldiers did, whether I would survive this battle and other conflicts in my career. However, I could only worry about the present; I couldn't contemplate the future. I dragged my mind back to the urgent task in hand and kept working.

CHAPTER 21

The Allies Prevail

The Major called with some great news: reinforcements had arrived at last and attacked and taken a hill a few miles behind us towards Dimapur. They were now setting up a large artillery base there to support our efforts. Even though they were much further away than we were, their guns were still capable of protecting our men on the hills with great accuracy. They could also eliminate the enemy artillery positions which had been set up around Kohima and were having a devastating effect on our army.

The new base, called Zubza, was several times the size of our unit on Jotsoma and was a great boost to our efforts. Our unit had been too small for the huge task and we urgently needed this back up. We all felt much more confident that together, we could support our army better and win this important battle. The Major would be coordinating our efforts for maximum advantage.

By now, though, I felt very sick. Over the past few days, the rain had fallen in sheets without letting up and our latrines had flooded, covering a wide area with sewage. The monsoon season had started in earnest. As my symptoms worsened, I guessed this raw sewage was the source of my problems.

My sergeant noticed and called out a medic to have a look at me. It didn't take him long to decide that I had a bad case of dysentery and would need to step back from operations. I told him, and Dobie, that I couldn't do that as I was needed for essential work in defence of the Army.

The medic sighed and looked at me, his expression telling me he had heard these lines a thousand times before. Between him and Dobie, I didn't have much choice, even though I begged to be allowed to carry on for a few more hours, claiming we were at a crucial stage of the battle. As I put my foot down, I got them to agree that I could carry on for one more night, and then I would be taken off active duty.

The following afternoon, I knew my time was up. I could hardly stand and didn't know what was affecting me more: the extreme exhaustion or my illness. Dobie put his arm around my shoulders and led me away from the guns towards our tents. He told me that after nine days and nights of non-stop activity, I had to rest. He would take over and look after the men.

His words had an almost hypnotic effect on me and I felt my energy draining away as my eyes closed. My knees couldn't support me and I collapsed, remembering little more.

The following morning, my sergeant gave me the terrible news about the direct hit and the loss of half our men. I managed to get to my feet and stagger towards the guns, but my legs gave way again and I was taken back to my bed. The medic came and told me that my condition had deteriorated, and I would have to be evacuated when the opportunity arose.

I didn't know this at the time, but learned later that the men trapped in Kohima were at last being relieved. How they had kept going through the intense bombardment with a severe lack of sleep, food and water was a complete mystery. Many had been wounded several times, but they never gave up. Now at last the wounded were being taken away from the battlefield to safety, and then on to hospitals in Dimapur to the north. I was to be taken with them. I felt guilty because I wasn't wounded like they were and I believed I was being evacuated under false pretences. Of course I wasn't the only one.

When I finally woke up almost a week later, I still felt dreadful in both mind and body. The medics who visited me decided I had a bad case of amoebic dysentery. As they didn't have the facilities locally to look after me, I would be taken further into India for intensive care. I gave no reaction to their comments as I really didn't care what became of me.

I had failed and let my men down, escaping the danger area without being wounded. I had let my family down and my life had ceased to exist. As I lay there, I wondered if I could do anything to hasten my end. I thought about this for many hours; I had nothing else to fill my head. I asked an Indian nurse if she had something she could give me so that I could sleep forever.

She looked rather shocked for an instant, and then sad; I guessed she had been asked the same thing before. Looking around the ward at so many men with limbs ripped off and shredded guts, I was sure she had. She told me patiently that hospitals don't work like that and she was trained to save lives, not end them, and nothing would change that.

There were rows of men lying in beds in a huge tented area, and the heat and smells were truly awful. I felt sorry for all the doctors and nurses working there and hugely respected their dedication and patience with us. I didn't trouble her again.

I thought about my religious education and the beliefs and convictions of my parents. There was no doubt at all in their minds that there was a God above us and His Son Jesus would save us. He had promised us that there would be a place in God's heaven for us if we believed in Him, and we all fervently did. In my childhood, I'd had serious doubts, but now I had none at all. I wasn't worried about dying, but I prayed that my journey to Him would be quick and painless.

But it wasn't my time yet.

I looked around the ward again. Many of us had lost most of our body weight and it was almost comical to see rows of near skeletons lying side by side. We were too tired and dehydrated to talk or move around as we lay there, suffering in the intense heat. Most of the men were unconscious anyway. This was one of the most miserable and depressing times of my life.

Days later, a few of us were wheeled out to waiting ambulances and taken to a nearby airfield. Drifting in and out of sleep, I was vaguely conscious of a throbbing droning noise as we flew further into India. I was then driven a long distance. The drive seemed never ending, but finally we arrived at a hospital.

I was cared for in this hospital for many boring months, given endless drugs while attached to a drip as the Indian nurses tried to rehydrate me. I was desperate for news from our men in Kohima; I'd heard about the long-awaited rescue by the British Second Division, but progress was still slow. Our exhausted men had been relieved at last, though, and that raised my spirits a little.

The new force was attacked by the enemy as the regiments had been before them and the struggle dragged on with the Allies finally gaining the advantage. However, the enemy refused to surrender. Our men had to bring up tanks to blast them out of their well-protected bunkers, and at last they were in retreat and the road south to Imphal was opened.

There is no doubt that Kohima was one of the fiercest battles our Army had ever had to endure, and it was a miracle that we not only held out against enemy masses, but overcame them. Kohima has since been compared to the terrible battle of Thermopylae in ancient Greece.

I wrote to Isla and it cheered me even further to receive a reply from her. Letters took weeks to arrive, so when I received one, I devoured it hungrily and replied almost immediately. Her father Henry was quite infirm as his heart condition had worsened. Her mother, the formidable Dr Jenny, was now running their two practices and insisted that Henry was not involved in the work at all. Despite her efforts, though, he managed to find out about the condition of many of his former patients and would infuriate her by advising her of the most appropriate treatments. Isla's work was going well, she said, but of course she was not able to discuss any details. I fully understood why.

After I'd spent four months in hospital, a doctor suggested that it was time for a period of rest and recuperation. I had not put on weight and was only a little over five stone; I found it extremely difficult to eat, and when I did, the food passed straight through my system. The medics tried to feed me with different foods, but nothing seemed to work and there was little I enjoyed eating. As a result, I was very weak; I had difficulty walking and hadn't even tried to climb the stairs.

The doctor told me that I needed to regain mental strength and normality (but what was normal?). I had fierce flashbacks and horrible images of my weeks in Kohima, shocking nightmares which depressed me and left me dazed and demoralised. He told me I had spent hours staring at nothing in particular and hadn't communicated much with other patients and staff. He suggested a long period of convalescence, and when I agreed, he told me about a tea plantation he had sent men to before. He said that the fresh air and work would help my fitness and be a great boost to my wellbeing.

I was to leave this wretched place at last! I was so pleased to have the opportunity. Within days, I was driven to the plantation several hours away. The owner was a British veteran who was sympathetic to soldiers who had suffered in the conflict. I spent several happy weeks there, and as soon as I was able to, I started to work on the land. Only an hour or two to start with, and then half days.

To make life even more pleasant, the owner had an attractive daughter and we enjoyed many hours in each other's company. Sometimes we didn't talk much, if at all, but this didn't seem to matter to either of us. I was very attracted to her, and I believe she was to me, too, but I was reluctant to take matters further as I had made a commitment to Isla. Nevertheless, I am sure my mental welfare benefited hugely from the friendship.

I thrived in the healthy hot climate and the work helped me regain my strength. Although its repetitive nature could be considered boring, to me, it was lifesaving. My fitness was improving, but I was still having difficulty holding my food and getting much needed nourishment. But it was almost time for me to resume my duties; there was a shortage of men for the campaign, especially those who had training and experience in battle.

As soon as I was ready, I flew to Burma where the enemy was in full retreat. Our mission was to rid the country of the Japanese and remove them as a threat to India. I spent several months in further combat, but unfortunately, I once again succumbed to the dreadful dysentery and reluctantly had to return to India for recuperation. While the Allied world was finally ringing with the jubilation and celebrations that heralded VJ day and the ultimate end of World War II, I was lying in a hospital bed, desperately ill.

Aftermath

Henry died just after the end of World War II and Dr Jenny, his widow, sold the two doctors' practices and retired to the south coast. She continued to be a formidable and forthright lady and lived for a further twenty-five years in a hotel.

Philip finally returned from India to England weighing just six stone (the effects of the dysentery stayed with him until his dying day). After a period of recuperation, he was sent to Palestine for peace-keeping duties. He loathed his time there, and after two years returned to England.

Philip and Isla were married on his return. They both had good lives and produced four happy and healthy children. I am their eldest boy.

Bibliography

Aslet, C: *The Birdcage: A novel of Salonika*. First Isis Edition, 2016. First Published by Cumulus Books, 2014

Deacon, A: *Diary of a Wren 1940–1945: War years in the Women's Royal Navy Service*. The Memoir Club, 2001

Deary, T: *Blitzed Brits (Horrible Histories Handbook)*. Scholastic Children's Books, 2009

Edwards, L: *Kohima, The Furthest Battle: The Story of the Japanese Invasion of India in 1944 and the 'British-Indian Thermopylae'*. The History Press, 2009

Fields, N: Thermopylae *480 BC: Last Stand of the 300*. Osprey Publishing, 2007

Fowler, W: *We Gave Our Today: Burma 1941–1945*. Weidenfeld & Nicholson, 2009

Furst, A: *Spies of the Balkans*. Wiedenfeld & Nicolson, 2011

Gilbert, V: *The Romance of the Last Crusade:* D. Appleton and Company, 1923

Holland, J: *Burma '44: The Battle That Turned Britain's War in the East*. Transworld Publishers (part of Penguin Random House), 2016

Kirkwood, K: *The Mystery of Isabella and the String of Beads: A woman doctor in WWI*. Loke Press, 2016

MacLean, A: *HMS Ulysses*. Harper Collins Publishers Ltd, 1955

Monsarrat, N: *The Cruel Sea*. House of Stratus (an imprint of Stratus Books Ltd), 1951

Page, G: *We Kept the Secret: Enigma Memories*. George R Reeve Ltd, 2002

Paterson, M: *Voices of the Code Breakers: Personal Accounts of the Secret Heroes of World War II*. David and Charles Ltd, 2007

Rooney, D: *Burma Victory*. Cassell & Co, 1922

Woodward, DR: *Forgotten Soldiers of the First World War*. Tempus Publishing, 2007

Milton Keynes UK
Ingram Content Group UK Ltd.
UKHW040748181023
430769UK00004B/133